Enrollment Form

☐ *Yes!* I WANT TO BE A *PRIVILEGED WOMAN*.
Enclosed is one *PAGES & PRIVILEGES*™ Proof of
Purchase from any Harlequin or Silhouette book currently for
sale in stores (Proofs of Purchase are found on the back pages
of books) and the store cash register receipt. Please enroll me
in *PAGES & PRIVILEGES*™. Send my Welcome Kit and FREE
Gifts -- and activate my FREE benefits -- immediately.
More great gifts and benefits to come.

NAME (please print)

ADDRESS   APT. NO

CITY   STATE   ZIP/POSTAL CODE

PROOF OF PURCHASE
SAMPLE ONLY

**NO CLUB!
NO COMMITMENT!**
*Just one purchase brings
you great Free Gifts and
Benefits!*

Please allow 6-8 weeks for delivery. Quantities are limited. We reserve the right to
substitute items. Enroll before October 31, 1995 and receive one full year of benefits.

Name of store where this book was purchased_____

Date of purchase_____

Type of store:

    ☐ Bookstore   ☐ Supermarket   ☐ Drugstore

    ☐ Dept. or discount store (e.g. K-Mart or Walmart)

    ☐ Other (specify)_____

Which Harlequin or Silhouette series do you usually read?

_____

Complete and mail with one Proof of Purchase and store receipt to:

  U.S.: *PAGES & PRIVILEGES*™, P.O. Box 1960, Danbury, CT 06813-1960

  Canada: *PAGES & PRIVILEGES*™, 49-6A The Donway West, P.O. 813,
      North York, ON M3C 2E8

SR-PP5B

▼ DETACH HERE AND MAIL TODAY! ▼

"Trust me." Matt put his hands on Carrie's shoulders and smiled at her.

She'd trust him with her life—she had, many times—but with her heart? She was intensely aware of his broad fingers sending shivery sensations up and down her body.

"I do trust you," she assured him, "but we need to get our act together before we meet the town council tomorrow. What's the plan?"

His answer was to slide his hands down her arms and leave them resting on her bare thighs. She tried not to notice, but the only time he'd ever been this close to her was in her dreams.

The flicker in his eyes turned serious. She knew instantly he was going to kiss her. Her heart pounded like a drum.

When his lips met hers, hard and sure, she was flooded with feelings she'd kept hidden all these years. But she couldn't let go. Because deep down she knew that Matt was just playing a part.

Dear Reader,

This month, take a walk down the aisle with five couples who find that a MAKE-BELIEVE MARRIAGE can lead to love that lasts a lifetime!

Beloved author Diana Palmer introduces a new LONG, TALL TEXAN in *Coltrain's Proposal*. Jeb Coltrain aimed to ambush Louise Blakely. Her father had betrayed him, and tricking Louise into a fake engagement seemed like the perfect revenge. Until he found himself wishing his pretend proposal would lead to a real marriage.

In Anne Peters's *Green Card Wife*, Silka Olsen agrees to marry Ted Carstairs—in name only, of course. Silka gets her green card, Ted gets a substantial fee and everyone is happy. Until Silka starts having thoughts about Ted that aren't so practical! This is the first book in Anne's FIRST COMES MARRIAGE miniseries.

In *The Groom Maker* by Debut author Lisa Kaye Laurel, Rachel Browning has a talent for making grooms out of unsuspecting bachelors. Yet, *she's* never a bride. When Trent Colton claims he's immune to matrimony, Rachel does her best to make him her own Mr. Right.

You'll also be sure to find more love and laughter in *Dream Bride* by Terri Lindsey and *Almost A Husband* by Carol Grace.

And don't miss the latest FABULOUS FATHER, Karen Rose Smith's *Always Daddy*. We hope you enjoy this month's selections and all the great books to come.

Happy Reading!

Anne Canadeo
Senior Editor, Silhouette Romance

Please address questions and book requests to:
Silhouette Reader Service
U.S.: 3010 Walden Ave., P.O. Box 1325, Buffalo, NY 14269
Canadian: P.O. Box 609, Fort Erie, Ont. L2A 5X3

ALMOST A HUSBAND

Carol Grace

ROMANCE™

Published by Silhouette Books

America's Publisher of Contemporary Romance

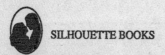

SILHOUETTE BOOKS

ISBN 0-373-19105-7

ALMOST A HUSBAND

Copyright © 1995 by Carol Culver

This edition published by arrangement with Harlequin Books S.A.

® and TM are trademarks of Harlequin Books S.A., used under license.
Trademarks indicated with ® are registered in the United States Patent
and Trademark Office, the Canadian Trade Marks Office and in other
countries.

Printed in U.S.A.

Books by Carol Grace

Silhouette Romance

Make Room for Nanny #690
A Taste of Heaven #751
Home Is Where the Heart Is #882
Mail-Order Male #955
The Lady Wore Spurs #1010
*Lonely Millionaire #1057
*Almost A Husband #1105

*Miramar Inn series

CAROL GRACE

lives with her inventor husband and two teenage children on a mountain overlooking the Pacific Ocean in California. From her house, she imagines she can almost see the Miramar Inn, the bed and breakfast owned by Mandy Clayton, the heroine of *Lonely Millionaire*, and visited by Carrie Stephens in *Almost A Husband*. Carol hopes her readers like the Miramar Inn series as much as she enjoys doing the research, clambering over the tide pools, strolling the wide beaches and watching the sun set into the sea. Miramar translates into "sea view" and she hopes that translates into "happy reading!"

Look for the third book in the Miramar Inn series sometime in 1996!

The Laws of Love according to Officer Carrie Stephens:

1. Never fall in love with a man you have to face danger with on a daily basis.

2. Never ask that man if he'll pose as your fiancé.

3. Never share the honeymoon suite with a man you're not *supposed* to be in love with.

4. Never let him go....

The Laws of Love according to Officer Matthew Graham:

1. Never get married—unless you are pretending, of course.

2. Never share the honeymoon suite with a woman you've never seen out of uniform.

3. Never let her know that you're having some very real feelings during those "make-believe" kisses.

4. Never let her go....

Chapter One

Life's A Bowl Of Pits. Somebody Else Got All The Cherries read the sign over Lt. Matt Graham's office door in the North Hollywood Police station. He didn't remember when he'd put it there, but he did remember that he'd left the door unlocked when he'd gone out to lunch, and now he had to use his key to get back in. He swung the door open quietly, so quietly his partner Carrie Stephens didn't hear him. She had the telephone cradled against her shoulder, her back to him, and was twisting a lock of auburn hair around her finger, something she usually did when she was worried or stressed.

"Of course I understand, Tony," she said in a tone so low he had to strain his ears to hear. "But I wouldn't ask if I thought you wouldn't enjoy it. Think about it—a vacation at a bed and breakfast along the coast."

Matt almost dropped his beat pack, the small suitcase with his radio, camera and shotgun shells. Carrie was begging some guy to go somewhere with her? He'd never thought much about her personal life. Never asked her anything. Respected her privacy the way she respected his. He assumed there were men in her life. She was young, attractive and bright. So why was she reduced to this? What was going on?

"Really," she continued, "it's okay. I can get someone else. Don't worry about it." Then she hung up. Her shoulders slumped and her red-gold hair tumbled forward. She sighed deeply and reached out to draw a line with her pencil through a name on a long list.

Matt cleared his throat, and she jumped a mile. When she whirled around he saw her blue eyes were suspiciously red around the rims. "I didn't hear you come in," she said, getting to her feet.

"Public Safety 101—How To Catch Your Suspect Unawares."

"I failed that one," she explained with a wry smile. "As you know, I always manage to cough or sneeze at the wrong time."

"Maybe you're just allergic to me," he suggested, hoisting his pack on top of his desk before sitting down behind it.

She shook her head. "It's the smog. That's part of the reason..." She broke off. He looked up. Their eyes met. She tore her gaze away. "There's something I have to tell you," she said.

He drew his eyebrows together in a frown. Whatever it was, it didn't look like good news. She leaned back against the edge of her desk. "I've been offered a job," she said, her eyes focusing on a crack in the plaster above his head.

"You've *got* a job," he answered.

"A better job. In administration. Chief of Police."

"Chief of Police?" He didn't mean to sound incredulous. He didn't mean to insult her. But he couldn't help being surprised. She was five years younger than he was. With five years less experience.

"In a small town," she explained. "So small you've never heard of it. At least, I hadn't. But it's perfect. On the coast, away from the smog, away from the violence. The worst thing that's happened there in twenty years was a woman hitting her husband over the head with a frozen lasagna."

He stared at her, unable to comprehend how she could even consider leaving L.A. "Oh," he said stiffly.

"The chief of police gets a furnished house, rent-free, an office in the library building, a secretary, and a deputy."

"What does he . . . she need all that for?" he asked. "If nothing ever happens."

"To prevent crime. That's the thing. To keep the crooks and the gangs out of the area and to create an atmosphere of security. With neighborhood watches, drug awareness programs in the schools . . . you get the picture."

"I get the picture. The picture of you dying of boredom in some backwater town."

Her eyes flashed the way they did when some lowlife was jerking her around. "I'd rather die of boredom than a bullet in the head."

"That's your choice."

"Yes, it is." She sat down hard on her swivel chair. "You couldn't be jealous, could you? Because I got the job and you didn't?"

"Jealous? Because you're moving to the sticks where you can't get a decent cup of espresso, or go to a concert or an art museum . . ."

She let her mouth fall open in surprise. "When was the last time you went to an art museum?" she asked.

"So I haven't gone. But I know I could go if I wanted to."

"Moss Beach has potential. They're starting to attract tourists for the scenery and . . . and . . . and one of these days they might even open a coffeehouse. Who knows?"

"*I* know you're trying to talk yourself into this. Why? Is it something I've done, something I've said? You don't want to be partners anymore? We can fix that. You don't have to move a thousand miles away."

"Six hundred. It has nothing to do with you." The minute she'd uttered the words, Carrie knew it wasn't true. It did have something to do with him. It had everything to do with him. She couldn't sit by any longer and watch the violence and the mean streets do their number on her partner. They'd taken a basically nice guy and turned him inside out. It wasn't only the violence. It was also his divorce. But despite the changes in him, despite the difference between what he once was and what he was now, she still felt, couldn't help feeling . . .

"Then what *does* it have to do with?" he asked, leaning back on two legs of his chair and crossing his hands behind his head.

"Me and my future. I'm almost thirty, Matt. I can't see myself at fifty still risking my life for a city that doesn't care."

He stared at her as if he were trying to picture her with gray hair and crow's-feet at the corners of her eyes, and she felt her cheeks redden under his sharp scrutiny. "And up there, wherever it is you're going, they care?"

"They care enough to invite me up there for two weeks, to stay at a bed and breakfast, all expenses paid, just to be sure I like it and they like me."

"And you're going?"

"Of course I'm going." Just let somebody try to stop her.

He slanted a sideways look at the list on her desk. "By yourself?"

She bit her lip. How much had he heard? What did he know about her fruitless search for someone to go with her? Suddenly she was tired of putting up a front. Of keeping her problem to herself. "Not exactly. I'm taking someone with me. My...my fiancé."

The front legs of his chair came crashing to the floor. "Who?"

She avoided his gaze. The tone of his voice told her all she needed to know. He didn't believe she had a fiancé. He didn't believe she *could* have one. He thought of her as a police officer, his partner, his buddy. But not as a woman, who might have a life after work, who might have a fiancé or at least a boyfriend. "All right," she admitted. "I don't have a fiancé. But they think I do. Is that so terrible?"

Matt stood and scrutinized a Wanted poster that had been on the wall for two months. "That depends. How did it happen?" he asked.

Carrie pressed her palms together. "They asked if I was married. I said no, not yet. That's all I said. But they jumped to conclusions. And the next thing I knew they were inviting me...and *him* to Moss Beach to see how we would like it." She looked at Matt, studied the way his uniform fit his broad shoulders, the way his dark hair, a shade too long to meet regulations, brushed the collar of his shirt, and she swallowed hard. How much longer could she keep her feelings for him a secret? He had an uncanny way of seeing beneath the surface, of reading people's minds. It was getting harder and harder to pretend.

"Do you *want* to get married?" he asked, keeping his back to her.

"No, I don't want to get married," she said a little too vehemently. "Of course I don't want to get married. I want the job. And if it takes a fiancé to get it, I'll get one." She hoped she sounded more confident than she felt. Because as of now she had absolutely no prospects. She'd run through her list backward and forward and come up with nothing, no one.

Matt turned slowly and looked at her. "What happens to the poor guy?"

"The 'poor guy' gets an all-expense paid vacation in beautiful Moss Beach. And I get the job. I don't know why..." She trailed off, disconcerted by the way he was staring at her, his eyes the color of flint and twice as sharp.

"Why it's so hard to find somebody?" he asked, with a pointed look at the list on her desk.

She covered it with the palm of her hand. "It's not that hard," she insisted. "I've just begun looking." If she'd learned one thing in her five years of arresting criminals, it was to keep denying the charges. No matter that the look in Matt's eyes told her he didn't believe her. How could he prove she was lying? Unless he'd heard her conversation, seen her list and knew she was bluffing.

On the other hand, he could usually tell when someone was lying to him. Even the most hardened criminal had trouble hiding the truth from Matt Graham. But Carrie was determined. She *would* find somebody to go with her, and she *would* get this job.

"I know what you're thinking," she said. "You think it's dishonest of me to let them think I'm engaged when I'm not. Well, that's fine. You go ahead, walk the streets of Hollywood for the rest of your life, inhale the smog, face off with every dirtbag that exists and let it turn you into a robot. I'm getting out." Her voice rose. "One way or another." She told herself to calm down. She mustn't let herself get carried away. Matt would think she'd gone off the deep end, cracked under the strain.

Where was the partner he used to know, the woman who never got excited? Not even when they'd stood together under a barrage of rock-throwers one dark night in Griffith Park, scared stiff that any one of those rocks could have been fatal. She prided herself on never panicking, never freezing. Never losing her cool. And that's the way she wanted to be remembered, if he ever thought about her at all after she left.

"Have you seen it yet, this paradise by the sea?" he asked, breaking into her thoughts as he seated himself on the edge of her desk.

"Not yet," she said. "But I'm sure..."

"You're sure it's a combination of Frontierland and Fantasyland."

"I've never been to Disneyland," she confessed. "I wouldn't know."

"Never been..."

"I've been busy—working days and going to school nights to get my degree in public administration."

"So you could get this job. What if it's not what you think?" he asked. "What if the people are rednecks and the town smells like fish from the packing plant?"

"It can't be worse than a dead body that's been in a basement for three weeks in the middle of summer. Remember that? How we had to sit and wait for the medical examiner to come and pick it up. Don't tell me you're not tired of it, too. Don't tell me you haven't changed, either. I've seen what's happened to you, and I don't want it to happen to me."

"Are you saying," he asked slowly, "that you're leaving because you're afraid of turning out like me?"

"You and everyone else around here. I became a cop to serve and protect. But I can't do that here. Not without turning into a complete cynic. I've got to get out while I still have a few ideals left. Because every time we haul in somebody who gets his kicks out of somebody else's pain, I add another layer to the shell around myself so I can keep functioning. But the thicker the shell, the more out of touch I get. Not with other people, but with myself. I don't know who I am anymore."

"I know who you are," he said, reaching down to tilt her chin with his thumb. She peered at him through a sheen of unshed tears. "You're a good cop," he continued. "The best partner I've ever had, and you need a vacation. That's all."

Carrie dropped her hands to her desk and stared at him with disbelief. The combination of his calloused thumb against her chin and his cool gray gaze made her heart pound erratically. But he hadn't understood a word she'd said. Nothing. "You're the one who needs a vacation," she countered. "How long has it been, a year, two years?"

"Something like that." He slid off her desk and ran his hand through his hair. "All right, you talked me into it. I'll come to Moss Landing with you. I'll be your fiancé for two weeks."

"Beach. Moss Beach," she corrected automatically while her mind spun around in circles. "I don't get it," she blurted. "I thought you didn't want me to go. You said there were rednecks and a bad smell in the air. Now you're taking off two weeks to go to a place you know you won't like to help me get a job you disapprove of. What do you get out of it?"

"Just what you said. A vacation in beautiful Moss Beach. A chance to tour the fish-packing plant."

"Seriously," she said, standing and twisting her fingers together.

"Seriously, I have vacation time I'll lose if I don't take it."

"Aren't you afraid you'll die of boredom?"

He shrugged. "Not in two weeks. I wouldn't want to live there, though. And you won't, either. I guarantee it. Not after you see it. You don't want to spend your days tracking down petty thieves who steal hubcaps from cars or locking up women who assault their husbands with frozen lasagna, then sit down and eat the weapon for dinner. But for a week or two, why not? There ought to be some decent salmon fishing up there. But..." A momentary flicker of doubt crossed his face as he gazed into her troubled blue eyes. "Maybe you'd rather have someone else?"

There is no one else, she thought.

She didn't answer his question. She didn't need to. It was obvious she would rather have someone else. Anyone else. But he was the only one who could stop her from making a serious mistake with her life, and he would if he could. He owed it to her. She hadn't complained once over these past years. She'd stuck it out through his black moods, his injuries, even his depression over the breakup of his marriage. He knew what she meant about not wanting to turn out like him. He didn't want to, either.

Matt walked around the room, opened the window, inhaled the acrid smell of smog and closed it again. There was no chance of Carrie turning out like him. She had a freshness about her that couldn't be tarnished. She would get her opportunity to advance. She didn't need to leave town to do it. Not now when he needed her, counted on her for her calm presence, her poise in the face of danger. She would be wasted in a place like Moss Beach. And if she didn't realize it herself, then he would have no choice but to point it out to her. For her own good.

"When do we leave?" he asked, suddenly apprehensive. What had he done? He didn't want to be anyone's fiancé, even for a day, even if it wasn't for real.

"Next week. I thought I'd drive along the coast, stop along the way, but now..."

"But now you've got a fiancé to consider. What does *he* want to do, what does *he* think? Are you sure you want to go through with this?"

"I have no choice," she said grimly. "I've asked everyone else on my list."

"Was I even on it?" he asked.

She looked out the window at the brown grass, unwatered because of the drought. "No," she said.

He knew he wasn't. Still, it felt like she'd thrown a dart at his heart. Why he should care, he didn't know. They were partners, nothing more, nothing less. And he wanted to keep it that way. He didn't understand why she wasn't happy with the status quo. All that talk about the smog and being out of touch with herself, were those the real reasons?

"Cheer up," he said when she continued to stare out the window. "It could be worse. I could be the Zodiac killer. But I'm an upstanding member of the police force. Your partner. Former partner."

"I know, and I appreciate what you're doing for me. It's just..."

"You'd rather not get engaged to a cop. I don't blame you. Cops make lousy fiancés and even worse husbands."

"I didn't say that," Carrie protested. "Cops just require a little extra TLC, that's all." She studied him out of the corner of her eye, wishing she could smooth away the lines that furrowed his brow and ease the tension that knotted the muscles of his shoulders. All the things his wife used to do for him. Then again, maybe she hadn't. He never said anything. About anything. "Don't you think so?" she asked.

"I don't think about it," he said curtly. He didn't think about marriage because it made him feel sick with remorse and guilt. "I don't know about you," he said, grabbing his holster from the desk drawer, "but I've got work to do. We're still on the front lines, you know. This is not the time to relax. We're still working the most dangerous station in the country and one slipup could be our last. Remember our objective."

Carrie adjusted her vest and straightened her jacket. "To go home alive at night," she muttered. But that wasn't her only objective. She had another one. To go home alive, but not alone. Maybe, just maybe, by getting away from L.A.

and from Matt, she would find a special man with an ordinary job she could go home to at night.

A fresh start was what she needed. A chance to make a niche for herself. No partner to care about, to hurt for when things went wrong. If Matt chose to stay in L.A. that was fine with her. She was moving on. He wouldn't miss her. Not after he'd broken in a new partner. Sure, he would rather not bother. He would rather have her stay forever. But for all the wrong reasons.

As for her, the strain was getting to her. The strain of hiding her true feelings. She had to so she could do her job. So she could be Matt Graham's partner, to make him proud of her, to earn his respect. Well, she'd gotten his respect, but that was all. That was enough, she told herself. That was plenty. All she could expect. But not all she wanted.

She glanced at him as she gathered her hand-held radio and loaded her camera with film. Damn it, why did he have to be the toughest, the strongest, the best-looking cop in the whole district, maybe the whole state? Make that the whole country. He was also the kindest, the funniest. At least, he used to be. Before his wife had left him.

Carrie had been waiting these past two years for Matt to snap out of it, and she wasn't going to wait any longer. He was hopeless, and she would be hopeless, too, if she didn't get out now. Hopelessly in love with her partner. First he was married to Shelly. Now he was married to his job. She didn't know which was worse.

Matt was standing in the doorway, waiting for her, watching her with a strange expression on his face. Good thing he couldn't read minds, though sometimes she wondered. In all her wildest dreams she'd never thought he would help her get a job by pretending to be her fiancé. She had the rest of the week to get used to the idea. And to try to figure him out.

One thing was for sure. He never pretended to be anything he wasn't. Not before this. So why start now? Why do something to help her do something he disapproved of? She shouldn't let him do it. She had a nagging feeling she would live to regret it. But if he didn't do it, who would? No one. She walked past him, out into the cold, cruel world for one of the very last times as Matt Graham's partner.

Chapter Two

Monday was one of those days when the smog hung over the Los Angeles basin like a big, thick, dirty blanket. There were warnings for seniors and children to stay inside and for joggers not to run for fear of damaging their lungs. In short, it was a good day to leave L.A. If it hadn't been, Matt might have called it off. Carrie was right, he hadn't had a vacation in more than two years. And he didn't need one now. His work was his life. The station was his home as much if not more than the efficiency apartment he'd moved into after his divorce.

When Carrie came by to get him, she looked around curiously at the bare four walls and then at him. He anticipated her question and answered it.

"Yes, this is where I live and, no, I'm not going to do anything with it. This is the way it came and this is the way it stays."

"Did I say anything?" she asked.

"You were going to."

"Do you have many guests?"

"None." He picked up his duffel bag. "Let's go."

He followed her down the stairs, watching her hips sway in khaki shorts, wondering if he'd ever seen her legs before. If he had he would have remembered, he decided. Long and slender. Funny how he'd never noticed. Her hair shone red-gold in the pale sunlight in front of his apartment and brushed the shoulders of her stretch T-shirt. He had a hard time tearing his eyes away for a minute. The way the shirt clung to her uplifted breasts was disconcerting. Not to him, of course, but what about the mayor and the city council or whoever it was she hoped to impress?

What kind of an impression did she want to make on her new town? Didn't she want them to recognize her brains and her skills? Who was going to notice when she was wearing this provocative outfit?

"We go straight to the bed and breakfast when we get there," she said. "The Miramar Inn has been written up in travel articles, and they say it's booked weeks in advance. We're lucky to get in... on the edge of the sea, very romantic..." She trailed off and gazed up the street, looking slightly uncomfortable.

"We'll take my car," he said, "and put yours in my garage. That way..."

"You can leave when you want to."

He nodded. "I'll ship yours up there if you decide to stay."

"Not if, *when*," she said, unloading her luggage from the trunk while he brought his car around to the front of the building.

So she'd dressed comfortably for the eight-hour ride, he told himself as he headed for the freeway, and not to tantalize him. No one had tantalized him for so long it took him a half hour to realize that's what was happening. And it wasn't just the clothes and her slim, shapely body. It was her red hair, blowing in the wind like a flag and smelling like sunshine.

With the top down the car flew down the freeway. He didn't know what she was thinking about behind her dark sunglasses, but she must be glad to put the dirty air behind them. He was, though it was strange not to be going to work. Not to be wearing a uniform, not to be anticipating danger on the streets.

Instead he was anticipating...what? Matt glanced at Carrie, studying her profile surreptitiously and wondering for the hundredth time in the past few days why he'd volunteered for this job. Now it wasn't so bad being alone in the car with her, with the wind rushing past his ears, the noise preventing them from talking. But he wondered what in hell they would talk about when it was quiet.

They'd never had trouble making conversation before. But that was about work. This was...something else. Work was fading into the background. How in hell would they convince people they were engaged? When they stopped in the charming town of Solvang for Danish pastries and coffee, he would ask her.

"I don't know," Carrie said. "I hadn't thought about it." Hadn't thought about it? She hadn't thought about much else. How did people act when they were engaged? Matter-of-fact? Disgustingly adoring? Mushy? She gave a little shiver of concern.

"Don't worry, I'll handle it," Matt assured her, adding a packet of sugar to his coffee.

She met his gaze hesitantly. "You will?"

"Sure. So you can concentrate on your interviews or whatever. I'll do the fiancé thing."

"Well...all right, fine. At least you've had experience in that department."

He grimaced. "Don't remind me."

"I'm sorry."

"So am I."

Carrie hesitated. If she didn't ask him now, she might never get another chance. "What happened?"

"To my marriage?" He braced his hands against the small round table and looked into her eyes. But his expression was blank. His eyes were the color of steel. "Nothing," he said. "Let's go."

She set down her half-finished coffee and followed him to the car. If she'd thought everything would be different once they'd left L.A., she was mistaken. He'd shut her out of his past just as effortlessly as he'd done back in L.A. She could spill her guts all over the sidewalk and still Matt would hold everything inside. She couldn't imagine what it would take for him to shake loose the past and let it go. A more powerful force than herself, that was for sure. Maybe an earthquake, something around the magnitude of 8.6. Something that would turn the Dorothy Chandler Pavilion into rubble, send the Pacific Coast Highway sliding into the sea. Maybe, just maybe, that would jar some of those awful secrets loose.

The next stop was a late lunch at Big Sur. At the restaurant perched on the side of a cliff overlooking the ocean below, they sat outside on the deck. Carrie inhaled the clear cool air and tilted her face toward the sun.

"You like it here," he observed from across the table.

"I love it here," she said. "Don't tell me you don't appreciate the air and the view..."

"The absence of gunfire," he finished. "Sure I do. But I wouldn't want to live here. What would you do after lunch? Where's the challenge? The reason to get up in the morning, to get the blood pumping?"

She sighed. "I thought you'd wait till we at least got to Moss Beach before you started. Besides, we're on vacation, so we don't have to do anything after lunch. Just keep driving. And you're not going to live there, so stop worrying about it. You'll be on your way back home before long. If you can call your apartment home," she added.

"What's wrong with my apartment?" he asked.

"It looks like no one lives there. Why don't you put something on the walls, like pictures?"

"Of who?"

"Of you, of your family." She watched him from behind her sunglasses, realizing how seldom she'd seen him in civilian clothes. She noticed how well the polo shirt fit across his broad chest, wondering idly who'd picked it out for him. Wondering who'd pressed his slacks. Realizing how little she knew about him, in spite of the years they'd worked together. Imagining that the lines around his mouth had softened since they'd left town. Wishing for the impossible.

He shook his head. "No family," he said.

She let that pass. "Then what about those pictures of you in the newspapers, the articles, your awards?" she continued. "Where are they?"

"In a box in the closet. What do you want me to do, paper the walls with them?"

"Other people do."

"I'm not other people."

"That's for sure." She ordered a chicken salad with walnuts and grapes and a glass of ice tea. Then she turned her chair toward the sea to admire the sparkling water below and ignore the man across the table who was determined to keep his feelings as well as his mementos in a box in the closet.

Let him keep his past locked away, let him live out his life alone. She didn't care. He wasn't her responsibility. She was only responsible for herself. But suddenly she was worried. What if he was right? What if there was no challenge, no reason to get up in the morning? What if there was no special man with an ordinary job who could compete with the extraordinary man she'd been working with these past years?

Then she would just grit her teeth and bear it. Because she was more certain than ever that she had to get away from him. From his cool gray eyes, from his strength, his savvy, his intelligence and his single-minded devotion to duty. If she stayed where she was, she would always be his partner, working in his shadow, and hopelessly, helplessly infatuated with him. Maybe she wouldn't be able to forget him in Moss Beach, but at least she would have a chance. She finished her salad, folded her napkin and they left the restaurant.

The towns were few and far between as they traveled north on the coast highway. The air grew cooler, the coastline more rugged. Matt pulled a natural-colored wool sweater over his head and Carrie wrapped a jacket around her shoulders.

"Want the top up?" he asked, and she shook her head. The mist that rolled in off the ocean smelled like brine and salt and curled her red hair into tendrils around her face. She got out the map and gave Matt directions. They turned off the highway at dusk in a heavy fog and the headlights picked up a sign carved into a piece of driftwood at the end of the driveway. Miramar Inn.

"This is it?" he asked dubiously.

"Yes," she acknowledged, peering through the fog at the rustic, brown-shingled house at the end of the driveway. "They say it's absolutely charming."

It *was* charming, she decided once she'd had a look at the living room with the fire blazing from the tiled fireplace. There was a bottle of sherry on the coffee table, a bowl of ripe pears and apples along with a round of Brie. Carrie met Matt's gaze and he nodded his grudging approval.

"Sit down," their obviously pregnant hostess said, indicating the love seat flanking the fireplace. "I'm Mandy Clayton and this is my husband Adam," she said gesturing to the man seated on the couch. "You must be the new police chief." She smiled at Matt and he shook his head.

"I am," Carrie said, accepting a glass of sherry.

"I'm sorry," Mandy gasped. "You must take me for a complete sexist. But I hope I didn't get it *all* wrong. You're Matt and Carrie and you're here on your honeymoon. They told me to reserve the suite."

Carrie choked on her sherry, and Matt looked like he'd swallowed the whole glass.

"We're just...engaged," Carrie managed to say when she'd found her voice.

"Oh, no." Mandy picked up the tray of cheese and fruit and offered it to her guests. "I feel absolutely terrible about this," she said, watching Matt cut a wedge of Brie and spread it on a cracker. "All I have left is the suite, and if you're not...I mean, some people are not adverse to having a honeymoon before the wedding, but I can't...I don't want...I'm sure Mayor Thompson told me you were married."

"She probably did," Carrie said reassuringly, though her mind was spinning with the complications that loomed. She had no idea what Matt was thinking, calmly eating his fruit and cheese as if it was all her problem. Which it was. "She'd prefer that I was married, but I'm not. Not yet," she added hastily.

"I understand perfectly," Mandy assured her. "The mayor is very traditional in some ways. Though she herself has broken the mold in being our first woman mayor. In other places that's not so unusual, but in Moss Beach, well...anyway, I think it's fabulous you're going to be our first woman chief of police."

"I hope so," Carrie murmured, sitting on the edge of the love seat. "Do you think the town is really ready for one?"

"As long as she's not a rabble-rouser. As long as she's a normal woman, if you know what I mean. With a fiancé like yours it should be no problem convincing anyone. But what do I know about it way out here in the boonies? I never thought *I'd* get married until my sister forced me to answer a personal ad in a magazine.'' Mandy glanced across the room at her handsome husband with undisguised admiration. ''I'm thrilled for you. And grateful for what you're doing for all of us. One giant step for womankind.''

''Thank you,'' Carrie said, eyeing the food with longing. If only her stomach would stop churning, she might try some. But she couldn't stop thinking about the honeymoon suite upstairs, imagining a heart-shaped bed, mirrors on the ceiling and a giant bathtub for two. She gave a little shiver, and Matt pulled her jacket up around her shoulders from behind her without missing a beat of his conversation with Mandy's husband. She didn't dare turn to look up at him. She was afraid she'd see accusations in his eyes, that his gaze would say, ''Look what you got us into.''

Yes, she knew what she'd gotten them into. But up till now the whole thing seemed possible—bringing Matt with her, passing him off as her fiancé. A challenge well worth the effort. But now that the pictures in the brochure had turned into a real inn, lovingly decorated with a honeymoon couple in mind, luring them to climb the stairs to the suite, enticing them to close the door behind them, to fling themselves in each other's arms, to peel their clothes off with reckless abandon, forget the world outside . . .

Carrie took a large gulp of the amber-colored sherry in her glass. Mandy was still smiling at her, still talking about the town and Carrie's job while Carrie wondered just how long she could prolong the cocktail hour. She didn't dare ask for another drink or she would lose what few wits she had left. Already her lips were numb, and her brain wasn't far behind. What if she excused herself, walked out the front door and never came back? Maybe they would think she got lost in the fog. Her gaze darted around the room, avoiding the staircase, as if it might disappear if she didn't see it.

Where was Matt? Had he done what she wanted to do? Walked out while he still had a chance? Maybe the back door was a better idea. Anything, *anything* but sharing a room with him. She looked out the bay window into the dusk and Mandy smiled understandingly.

"He went out to get your bags," the hostess explained.

Carrie nodded. Maybe he did go out to get the bags, or maybe he was fifty miles down the road by now heading for home. She couldn't blame him. It was one thing to sit around the office six hundred miles away planning a quasi vacation with your partner, and another to come face-to-face with a honeymoon suite and your partner, a partner who wore a blue uniform and was just one of the boys.

That's what he thought of her. She knew it. She'd always known it. It must have shaken him even more than her to hear about the arrangements. So much that he'd simply walked out. Why else didn't he come back with the suitcases? Carrie didn't realize she was staring at the front door and holding her breath until Matt walked through the door, one suitcase under each arm.

She stared at him as if she'd seen a ghost. Not the way one would look at one's fiancé, but considering the state of her nerves, she was lucky she hadn't screamed. She set her glass on the table and stood. She could say she was sick and had to go home. Maybe she *was* sick. Maybe that's why her hands were shaking and her knees were so weak she could hardly stand.

Matt was looking at her, his lips clenched in a straight line, the picture of a man waiting to be sentenced. She wanted to tell him she was sorry. To say she'd made a mistake, to grab her suitcase and run out to the car, but she couldn't move, couldn't speak. The look he gave her said it all. *I can't believe what you've done. Lured me here, trapped me into a fake honeymoon along with the fake engagement.*

Somewhere a voice penetrated her thoughts. It was Mandy, offering to show them to their room. Just the word "room" sent tremors through Carrie's body. Her eyes darted from Mandy to Matt. They were both watching her, waiting for her to speak. It was now or never. After an interminable wait she forced her mouth into a smile.

She didn't know how she managed to get up those stairs. But somehow with Mandy in the lead and Matt behind her, they all arrived at the door to the infamous honeymoon suite. *Suite,* Carrie thought desperately. That could mean two rooms. It could mean two beds. Two beds for a honeymoon? No way. Mandy flung open the door and waited anxiously. Carrie's heart fell. She pressed her hand against her chest to stop her pounding heart, and exclaimed how nice it was. It *was* nice. If you liked honeymoon suites.

If you liked brick fireplaces, ready for a cozy fire; if you liked antique oak chests and padded window seats made for two. Then there was the bed, one enormous bed, covered with a thick, mile-high comforter and pillows piled invitingly at the headboard.

Suddenly Carrie's knees buckled, and she reached for the round-carved post at the foot of the bed. But instead of the bedpost, her hand met Matt's and he held her tightly by the wrist.

"You okay?" he asked, watching her eyelashes flutter against her cheeks.

"Fine," she said, grateful for the support. Grateful to him for not protesting, at least not in front of their hostess. "It's really lovely," she told Mandy truthfully.

"You're sure you don't mind?" Mandy asked, poised in the doorway, her expression anxious.

"Not at all," Matt said firmly, pulling Carrie to him, her back against his chest, and cupping her elbows in his palms. Her spine stiffened.

Mandy sighed with relief then carefully closed the door behind her.

As soon as she was gone Carrie moved away from Matt and sat on the edge of the bed with her face in her hands. She could hear Matt walking around the room, but she didn't dare look at him. She'd promised him a vacation, but she'd put him in a compromising position, an embarrassing situation. She'd never dreamed of what it would take to convince the town she was engaged, and was seriously beginning to doubt whether she could go through with it.

Carrie heard Matt approach the bed. She felt the mattress give as he sat next to her, so close his thigh pressed against hers. His shoulder brushed hers, the heat from his body rushing through her. She raised her head and looked at him. The expression in his eyes surprised her. Amusement lurked in the depths. That and something else. It wasn't anger, it wasn't embarrassment.

"I'm sorry about this," she said, wondering why he sat so close to her when the bed was so big, so soft, so inviting. "This . . . honeymoon business."

He shrugged. "Don't worry about it. I said I'd handle it and I will. Trust me." He put his hands on her shoulders and smiled at her as if this was nothing more than a slight procedural glitch in regulations.

Trust him? She would trust him with her life, she had many times, but with her heart? She looked away for fear he would read her thoughts. She was intensely aware of his broad fingers sending shivery sensations up and down her body.

"I do trust you," she assured him. "But I want to know what the plan is. We need to get our act together before we meet the town tomorrow." She paused. "What is the plan?"

He slid his hands down her arms and left them resting on her bare thighs. She tried not to notice. She tried to act as casual as he did, but the only time he'd ever been this close to her, touching her bare skin, was in her dreams. This wasn't a dream. It was real. But it wouldn't last.

Just then the flicker in his eyes turned serious. He turned his head, and she knew instantly he was going to kiss her. Her heart pounded like a jungle drum. She raised her arms, whether to push him away or wrap them around him she didn't know. She just knew if her heart pounded any louder it would wake the other guests as he came closer, a fraction of an inch at a time until his face blurred before her eyes.

When his lips met hers, hard and sure, she was flooded with feelings she'd kept hidden all these years. All the need and want and desire trembled on the verge of discovery. But she couldn't let go. Because deep down she knew that Matt was playing a part. He was a man who never let go, who never lost control. Who was making her lips tingle while he teased her. She wanted to give in to the kiss, to part her lips and throw herself into it, but first she had to know, what was this all about?

With a burst of willpower she pulled back and looked at him. He was breathing a little too hard for a man in complete control. And yet... "What are you doing?" she whispered.

"Just what you said. Getting our act together." He ran his hand along her cheekbone, then brushed her lower lip with his thumb.

"Of course," she said with a shaky laugh. "Our act." She told herself she'd almost lost her head. Almost believed it was for real. And just because of a little heavy breathing. I mean, how naive could she get?

"That's the kind of thing that will convince anybody," he remarked.

Even herself. That's how desperate she was. She stood and walked around the bed, wondering why she hadn't brought someone else, someone she could love and leave. "But I'm not sure who we have to convince here tonight," she said, matching his casual tone.

"We're practicing," he said from the edge of the bed.

"At night?"

"Day and night until we get it right," he said.

Get *what* right? she wondered. Her gaze returned to the bed and with it, her thoughts. Thoughts of spending the night there with him. She wrapped her arms around her waist. "In case you're worried," she said, avoiding his gaze, "I plan to sleep on the floor." Might as well clear the air, which had become thick with tension.

Matt raised his eyebrows. "And have them saying the honeymoon was over before the wedding? I wouldn't advise it." He walked over to the window and peered out into the darkness. "Unless you've had enough of this one-horse town. It looks pretty remote out there to me, no lights, no neighbors, no noise. What do you think?"

She could have joined him at the window, rested her head on his shoulder while they gazed out into the night together as lovers would, but she didn't. For him it was all an act, for her it was all too real.

"So far I think it's perfect," she insisted. "And I haven't seen anything yet, the house or the town or the beach. I think I'm going to love it." Whether she loved it or not, she was not going back to be Matt Graham's partner. She was going to get this job if she had to make love with Matt on the steps of city hall to prove to the town that they were engaged and that she was the woman for the job.

The thought brought a flush to her cheeks as she pictured the crowd gathered around to watch the spectacle. Would they be thrown in jail? Would she have to arrest herself for indecent exposure and lascivious behavior? She suppressed a giggle. She was on the edge of hysteria.

"What is it?" he asked with a puzzled look.

"Nothing. I think I'll get ready for dinner." She unzipped her suitcase, grabbed some underwear and a dress and headed for the bathroom.

Matt stood with his back to the window, staring at the closed bathroom door, listening to the water run in the tub, feeling as if he'd been hit over the head by a wino with an empty bottle, something that had happened to him twice in his career. What had made him kiss Carrie, his friend and his partner? Was it the warm room, the soft bed, the mist outside? Was it the smell of her hair or the satin-smooth feel of her skin under his calloused hands? The kiss had shocked him, forced him to reexamine his feelings.

He turned and pressed his head against the windowpane. No, it was just what he'd said. It was acting. It was just helping her get the job she wanted, though why he should help her leave him to break in someone new, he didn't know. Maybe it would all work out for the best without his help. He could only hope the mayor would be a tyrant, the house a dump, and the beach littered with cans and broken bottles. Because if it wasn't, he would have to think of another way to talk her out of this crazy idea. Or maybe talk the town out of the crazy idea of a woman police chief.

In the meantime he would be the world's best fiancé—supportive, kind and loving. A man for the nineties. Everything he hadn't been in the past. Then when it fell through, she couldn't blame him. When she decided on her own that Moss Beach wasn't the right place for her and Los Angeles was, he would be there to tell her she'd made the right decision.

When Carrie finally came out of the bathroom, Matt sucked in a deep breath. He'd seen her out of uniform only rarely. Tonight there was no bulletproof vest to restrain her breasts. There was even the hint of a lacy bra at the décolletage of her neckline, and the silky fabric clung to her hips. He told himself to calm down. It was his turn for a shower, and as he stood under the shower with the cold water coursing down on his back, he told himself not to do anything he would be sorry for later. Because if all went according to his plan, they would be partners for a long time. Back where they belonged.

He got out of the shower and toweled off. A cosmetic bag was on the counter. Next to a bottle of shampoo. He picked up the bottle and inhaled the scent of honey and almonds. Carrie's scent.

There was a knock on the door. Matt gripped the towel around his waist and set the shampoo down with a thump.

"I'll meet you downstairs in the living room," Carrie said. "I want to ask Mandy some questions."

He didn't say anything, but he wondered. Was one of the questions, Can I have a roll-away bed brought in? He never found out.

When he'd dressed in khakis, a shirt, tie and a corduroy jacket, he went downstairs to find Carrie had obtained the directions to a seafood restaurant nearby. They said good-night to their hostess and went outside into the fog.

After a short, quiet ride they arrived at a low, Cape Cod-style building with gray shingles that blended into the landscape.

Inside the restaurant, Matt said, "If we were really en-gaged, we'd ask for a quiet table in the corner."

She shrugged and asked the maître d' for a quiet table in the corner. When they were seated, they ordered a Califor-nia Chardonnay. When it arrived, Matt said, "If we were really engaged, we'd drink a toast."

Carrie hesitated for only a moment. Then she lifted her glass. "To us," she said in a husky voice that didn't sound at all like her.

He studied her for a long moment, noticing the way the candlelight picked up the highlights in her hair. "You're getting good at this," he said, touching his glass to hers.

She glanced around the room. "You never know who might be at the next table. Some pillar of society or a local official. I can't be too careful."

"You really want this, don't you?"

"More than anything."

"And you'd do anything to get it?"

"Anything," she assured him.

"Even marry me?"

She drew in a quick, sharp breath. "That won't be necessary."

"What's going to happen when I go back to L.A.?" he asked, refilling her wineglass.

"I'll say you broke up with me. You didn't like it here, or something like that."

"What if I do like it here?" He was playing the devil's advocate, just to see what she would say. That was all. There was *no* chance he would like it here.

Carrie paused while the waiter prepared a Caesar salad at their table. When he'd divided the romaine lettuce, the croutons and the grated cheese onto two plates and added some freshly ground pepper, she continued. "You've already made up your mind, remember? You called it a backwater and a one-horse town. Besides, what would you do even if you liked it here, stay home and water the flowers? I'm not worried." She smiled and speared a lettuce leaf with her fork.

"Don't look now," he said under his breath, "but there's a couple across the room who are looking at us with more than normal curiosity."

"What'll we do?" she said, dropping her fork.

He reached for her hand, brought it to his lips and kissed her fingertips one by one. "How's this for a start?" he asked with a sideways glance at the couple.

"Very nice," she murmured.

"I saw it in a movie," he confessed. But in the movie the man had had no trouble keeping his hand steady while he'd kissed the woman's fingers. What was wrong with him, anyway? Was he still reeling from the shock of seeing Carrie in that sexy dress? Eating with her by candlelight? Watching her hair tumble over her shoulders? Wanting to take each curl between his thumb and forefinger and revel in its silkiness? If he felt this way during dinner in a crowded restaurant, what would happen afterward when they were back in their bedroom all alone? No more kisses. That was for sure.

He held on to Carrie's hand as the woman who was watching them finally got up and approached their table. "Excuse me," she said, "but I don't suppose you're the new police chief, are you?" This time the question was clearly for Carrie and not Matt. Reluctantly he let go of her hand.

"I am," Carrie said. "And this is my fiancé, Matt Graham."

The woman giggled. "I knew it. I said to Lionel, that's her. And he didn't think you looked like a police chief."

"I'm off duty tonight," Carrie explained. She smiled into Matt's eyes, and he felt that smile all the way down to the soles of his shoes. She wasn't just getting good at this, she was getting *great*. Who would have believed she didn't mean it?

"Tonight she's mine, tomorrow she belongs to the town," Matt said lightly, sliding one shoe off and nudging her leg with one stockinged foot, just to show her he could play the game as well as she could.

"Oh, my," the woman said. "Isn't that romantic? Well, I'll leave you two lovebirds alone and I'll see you tomorrow. I'm Sally Goodenhour, by the way, the mayor's secretary."

"Glad to meet you," Carrie said, shaking the woman's hand then watching her return to her table, collect her husband and leave the restaurant.

"You were right," Matt said, digging into his salad. "They're everywhere. You can't be too careful."

"I appreciate your help," she said. "You were very convincing." She held her wineglass to the light and gazed at it thoughtfully. So convincing he almost had her believing... "The foot under the table," she murmured, "that was a nice touch."

"Glad you liked it," he said with a grin.

"What movie was that from?"

"Give me some credit," he said, "for a few ideas of my own."

She swallowed hard, thinking of the night to come, of the days and nights, wondering what other ideas he had. Wondering how much of his behavior stemmed from a desire to help her get the job and how much was intended to distract her from getting the job. "Could I ask you something?" she said, watching the waiter whisk the salad plates from the table.

"What is it?" he asked, the wariness back in his eyes, his mouth set in a straight line.

"How come you're doing this for me? Truthfully, are you helping me get the job so you can get rid of me?"

"Get rid of the best partner I've ever had? No way."

The waiter was back with the main course. Already. At this rate they would be back at the inn in no time, facing that bed, facing each other.

"Then, why?" she asked, pushing a giant prawn around on her plate, stalling for time.

"You said I needed a vacation." He took a bite of Dover sole.

"Since when have you ever done anything I suggested?"

He set down his fork. "Can I ask *you* something? How come you didn't ask me to come along? Why wasn't I on your list?"

Carrie kept her eyes on her plate, on the pool of champagne sauce and the pasta, because if she looked at him he might guess the real reason. No one was better at shaking the truth out of suspects. Circling with innocuous questions until, before they knew it, they'd come clean and he'd had his confession. And they never knew what had hit them. "I didn't think you'd come," she said finally.

"You were wrong."

"Why did you?"

"To help you out. And I'm doing it, aren't I? Do you have any complaints? Or do you wish what's-his-name—Tony?—had come instead of me?"

"You're doing a great job," she assured him. "So far."

"So far? You think I can't keep it up? You think I'm going to let you down?"

She looked up at him. The edge in his voice surprised her. "You've never let me down before, but this is different. Do you think it's wrong to lie to them this way? Do you think it's immoral?"

He studied her for a long moment while she twisted her napkin in her lap, waiting for his judgment. "I guess the end justifies the means, as Plato said."

"Plato? Are you sure that wasn't Machiavelli?"

"Whatever."

He reached for her hand and covered it with his. Her heart contracted. A warmth stole through her body. And then she remembered. She glanced over her shoulder. Sure enough, a man a few tables away was craning his neck in their direction. She should have known. The gesture meant nothing. Except that Matt was on guard. As usual. On or off duty, his antennae were up. His instincts were right on target. He knew when he was being watched and why. And he reacted. Usually with his gun. This time by grabbing her hand. She ought to feel grateful. Instead she felt let down.

"Who could that be?" he asked.

"Probably the president of the school board. I don't want to know. I can't handle anyone else tonight. Can we sneak out of here?"

"Without dessert?" he asked.

"I'm not hungry."

"I'll get the check," he said.

"I'll put it on my credit card," she said.

"No, you won't. Do you want the man to see us fight over the check?" he demanded.

"Of course not," she insisted.

"Do you want the waiter to tell everyone in town you paid for dinner?"

She hesitated. "I think it's in keeping with my image."

"Well, it's not in keeping with mine."

She pressed her lips together and let him pay the bill. Who would have thought he would go all macho on her at a time like this? After years of splitting the bill. She would settle with him tomorrow. Right now she had other things to worry about. The inn, the room, the bed.

Chapter Three

The lights of Mandy Clayton's bed and breakfast glowed warmly through the fog. If it weren't for the bed problem, and the Matt problem Carrie would have looked forward to going up the stairs, getting into her flannel nightgown, snuggling under the down quilt and falling into a deep sleep. But as it was, the logistics of two people who were not romantically inclined—at least one of them wasn't—trying to get undressed and into bed, and actually *sleeping* there staggered the mind. All Carrie could think of was that after years of looking at Matt in a uniform she was now going to look at him without...without anything. Or much of anything.

While she fought off thoughts of his well-toned body without benefit of clothes, Matt parked in front of the big house, opened the door for her and was waiting for her to get out of the car. With a silent warning to keep her imagination in check, she made her way to the front door and found the living room full of people.

"Laurie, this is the new police chief, Carrie Stephens. And her fiancé," Mandy said to the woman next to her.

The slim, blond woman shook Carrie's hand and led her to the fireplace to warm up. "I'm Mandy's sister. I heard how they snagged you from La-la land, somebody with real experience. It's the most exciting thing to happen around here since the Pronzinis' honeybees got loose and descended on the nudist beach. Tell me," Laurie said eagerly, "what's it like down there? Do you drive a Ferrari that you seized from a drug dealer? Do you have quotas for tickets? Isn't your fiancé worried about you getting wounded in action?"

Carrie stared into the woman's friendly eyes and took a deep breath. "I drive an old Volvo. I've never seized anything from anybody. I'm not a traffic cop anymore, and my...um, fiancé is also a cop so he's aware of the dangers."

Carrie saw Laurie give Matt a swift appraisal. He was engaged in conversation with Mandy's husband. "He looks like something right out of Hollywood," she said admiringly.

"He is. But not the Hollywood you're thinking of. The behind-the-scenes Hollywood. It's pretty seamy and it's not on any tourist map of the stars' homes."

"Well, if he isn't a movie star, he should be. How does he feel about your taking the job? I guess I should ask him."

Carrie wanted to shout no, but before she could say anything, Laurie had traded places with Adam. Carrie watched anxiously as Laurie stood beside Matt and wished she could hear what he had to say about her. So far she couldn't fault him on his acting ability. If anything, he was a little too good at it. She had a hard time tearing her eyes away from her so-called fiancé, his tall frame leaning against the mantel, his face animated as he talked to the small group.

And she couldn't help imagining what it would be like if she *were* engaged to Matt and she *had* come to this charming B and B with him as her real fiancé. A tiny sigh escaped her lips.

"Your fiancé tells me you have quite an impressive record," Adam said, bringing Carrie back to earth. "First in your class at the police academy and later decorated for bravery. Of course, he *could* be prejudiced," he said with a warm smile. "I'm always bragging about Mandy, too. Did you know she decorated the rooms here herself? She just finished painting the honeymoon suite, how do you like it?"

Carrie was barely aware of the walls, let alone the paint on them, but she managed to say it was beautiful.

"You'll have to come back on your honeymoon," he suggested. "Or do you have other plans?" Carrie gulped and shook her head. How many more questions like this would there be? "We came here on our own honeymoon," he continued. "Closed the place up and had it to ourselves for once."

Carrie nodded, wondering how it would feel to have someone so in love with you his eyes lit up at the mention of your name. Mandy was lucky. So was Adam to have a wife who could decorate and cook and be a gracious hostess. Carrie could hit a target in practice, subdue a suspect using pressure points and negotiate a hostage release, but she'd had no success in finding herself a husband. It didn't matter. She didn't need one. She just needed a fiancé, and that was only temporary.

Her only goal was to get through the next two weeks without anyone finding out that Matt was only interested in retaining her as his partner. Anxiously she looked at him talking to the others in the corner, holding them enthralled with some story or other. Suddenly he looked at her and their eyes locked and held for a long moment. Then he glanced pointedly in the direction of the stairs and her pulse rate jumped. It's all part of the act, she reminded herself sternly. She excused herself, but she couldn't move toward the staircase.

She was rooted to a spot in front of the fireplace. It wasn't until Matt crossed the room and put his arm around her shoulders that she knew she'd passed the point of no return. It was bedtime. She wondered what were the chances of a tidal wave sweeping them both away.

"Thanks for rescuing me," she said under her breath as they mounted the stairs together. "You wouldn't believe the questions they asked. They wanted to know if I confiscated cars from drug dealers." She gave a shaky, hollow little laugh. He was holding her so tightly his hip rubbed against hers.

"That's nothing," he countered. "They wanted to know what I was going to do while you're at work."

"What did you say?"

"I said I'd go fishing. So now they're looking for a boat for me. Can you see me hauling in my nets at night?"

She turned her head in his direction, which was a big mistake. His eyes, his mouth, were too close, so close she couldn't breathe. She tried to picture him with a wool stocking cap and a navy blue pea jacket on a fishing boat...just to distract herself from replaying that kiss, that strange, awkward exploratory kiss that left her disappointed, frustrated... "What's wrong with fishing?" she asked, dragging herself back to the conversation.

"It's fine. For a day. But for a career? I'm a cop, in case you forgot."

At the door to their room, she tilted her head and looked up at him in the light from the hall fixture, at the lines etched in his forehead, the tension engraved around his mouth. "A burnt-out cop. Maybe you ought to think about getting out before it's too late."

"Leave me out of this," he said, his tone suddenly cool. "We're here to get you a job. I've already got a job. One I'm going back to as soon as I can."

She nodded and pushed open the door. She didn't need to be reminded he was counting the minutes until he could leave. Why had she brought him along? Because there was no one else. Why hadn't she come alone? Because she wouldn't have gotten the job. Without him, she wasn't going to get the job. With him, she might get the job, but go crazy along the way.

She sank down onto the bed while he paced around the large room. "If you want to go back now, I understand," she said.

He stopped pacing and stared at her. "Now? We just got here. It was a long drive here, and I'm tired." He glanced at the bed and reached for the top button on his shirt. Carrie felt the blood rush to her head while she looked around for someplace to hide. He was going to undress right in front of her and climb into bed. Oh, Lord, what had she done?

"I didn't mean right now." She stood and ran her damp palms down the sides of her skirt. "I just meant that if you want to bail out, I'll understand."

He was halfway down the row of buttons on his shirt, exposing a broad chest dusted with golden hairs when he stopped. "Have I ever bailed out on you? I said I'd help you out and I will. Unless you think I'm not doing a good job."

"You're doing a great job. What were you all talking about down there?"

He tossed his shirt on a chair in the corner. Carrie gasped silently but couldn't tear her eyes away from his broad shoulders with the angry red scar running diagonally across his clavicle, his trim washboard stomach, the hair on his chest turning darker as it disappeared below his belt. Instinctively she moved as far from him as she could, against the far wall, and braced her back against it.

"I told them about the time you and I pulled that guy over on the freeway when you first started. You asked him why he was speeding. He said, 'I wasn't. The car was.' You said, 'Didn't you realize you were going too fast?'"

Carrie smiled. "And he said, 'I forgot my glasses. I couldn't see the speedometer.' So I asked him how he could drive and he said, 'I can see *far away.*'"

Matt laughed, then he sobered. "We've been through a lot together."

"Yeah." She wrapped her arms around her waist and thought about the good times, the bad times and the scary times. And she realized that tonight was good and bad and scary all at once. While she was thinking, Matt went into the bathroom. Carrie grabbed her nightgown from her suitcase on the luggage rack and pulled her dress off over her head, before donning the voluminous granny gown. After buttoning it up to her chin, she jumped into bed, clinging to the far side of the king-size mattress.

Carrie tried not to stare at the door to the bathroom, to anticipate Matt's return, to worry about what he would or wouldn't be wearing. Instead she forced herself to breathe slowly so she wouldn't hyperventilate. But before Matt came out, there was a light tap on the door. Carrie jumped out of bed and opened the door just a crack. It was their hostess.

"Sorry to bother you," Mandy said softly, "but I forgot to put the mints on your pillow." She held out her hand and Carrie took them. "And I wanted to apologize again for the mix-up."

"That's all right," Carrie said with a glance over her shoulder. It wasn't as if she was wearing a slinky negligee, but she still wanted to get back under the covers before Matt reappeared.

"What time would you like breakfast?" Mandy asked.

"Oh, about eight, I guess. I have my first appointment at nine."

She was about to close the door when Mandy continued, "Swedish pancakes or eggs Benedict?"

"Pancakes," Matt said suddenly from over Carrie's shoulder.

Carrie wanted to say she would have the same, but her mouth wouldn't move. He was so close she could feel his warm breath against the back of her neck. Then she felt his hands on her shoulders, warm and strong, and she had to remind herself that he wanted no part of this. She nodded at Mandy and closed the door.

"She's gone," she said. "You can let go."

Matt turned her around to face him, but he didn't let go. He kept his hands on her shoulders. He let his gaze slide down her flannel nightgown, past the row of tiny buttons, over the swell of her breasts and down to her bare feet. "Is that what you're wearing to bed?"

"What's wrong with it?"

"Everything. It looks like something out of the *Farmer's Almanac.*"

"So?" she said while she nervously unbuttoned the top button and then buttoned it again.

He watched, fascinated, fighting the desire to rip the buttons off himself. "So is it really what you'd wear on a vacation with your fiancé?"

"I hadn't thought about it," she admitted.

"Obviously. Or you would have packed something sexy. But that gives me a chance to buy you something more appropriate."

"I hardly think they'll have a Victoria's Secret in Moss Beach."

"I'll find something. We don't want it all over town that you look like Mother Goose at bedtime. We want it all over town that I bought you a negligee."

She ducked under his arms and walked around him. "Why?"

"For your image."

"How will it get all over town?"

"Gossip," he said, resting his hand on his hips. "That's all there is to do in a small town."

She went back to her side of the bed. He noticed that she hadn't looked at him since he'd come out of the bathroom, as if she'd never seen a man in boxers before and didn't want to start now.

"How do you know so much about small towns?" she asked.

"I've lived in them. That's how I know what they're like. The gossip, the boredom, the lack of things to do. That's how kids get in trouble."

"As if they don't get in trouble in the city." She climbed under the covers and pulled the sheet up to her chin, clinging so close to the edge of the bed he was afraid she'd fall off. "Were you one of them?" she asked, looking straight ahead at the wall.

"I was in some trouble."

"That's why you've got a soft spot for juveniles."

"I haven't got a soft spot for anyone who breaks the law."

"If you say so," she agreed.

"Look," he said, walking to her bedside and forcing her to look up at him. "Every kid I get off the streets, out of the gangs, is one less kid I have to worry about. I'm just looking out for myself."

"Okay," she said, and closed her eyes.

For some reason that annoyed him. "Look at me," he said. She opened her eyes and squinted at him. "Do I look like the kind of cop who spends his weekends at the youth center, who adopts orphans and who hands out presents at the Christmas party?"

"No," she said softly. "You look like the kind of cop who eats nails for breakfast." This time her gaze traveled down his bare chest across the plaid boxers and down his legs.

Matt felt the heat rise up the back of his neck and turn his ears red. This was Carrie, he reminded himself, his partner, who'd seen him every day for the past two years. But in uniform. Always in uniform. In a bulletproof vest that prevented her from seeing too much, from knowing too much.

Without another word he crossed the room, flicked off the light switch and got into bed. He lay there, about as far from her as he could be and still be in the same bed. The same with his goal of talking her out of taking this job. He was about as far away from that as he could be. It seemed to be slipping away from him. Instead of taking the opportunities she'd given him to back out, to sabotage her, he kept thinking of ways he could help her. Brag about her to strangers, buy her sexy lingerie. What was wrong with him, why hadn't he left when she'd told him he could?

Because it was late. It was dark, and he was tired. He would never admit he was having too good a time to leave. That he enjoyed watching Carrie fidget with her buttons while he imagined what lay underneath. That he was looking forward to tomorrow. To seeing what she would wear. To hearing what she would say. She wasn't the same as she was in L.A. Neither was he.

"Carrie."

"What?" Her voice was as soft as the gossamer silk he imagined her wearing to bed.

"You're an attractive woman. How come you don't have a real fiancé?"

"I thought you said I looked like old Mother Goose."

"It's the nightgown. Not you."

"Thanks. Well, I guess it's because all I ever meet are criminals and cops. And I'm not going to marry either one."

He turned his head in her direction. "Who *are* you going to marry?"

"Probably no one. But if I did, he'd be a special guy with an ordinary job. Maybe a plumber or a well digger."

She shifted, and the honey-almond scent of her hair and her skin wafted his way. He gripped the edge of the sheet as his heart went into overdrive.

"Maybe even a fisherman," she continued dreamily. "Anybody who comes home at night in one piece. Who hasn't spent the day fighting off women on every corner. Who isn't afraid to talk about how he feels, who still believes in the goodness of mankind. Does that sound like too much to ask for?"

"No," he said. But it sounded like everything he wasn't. What was it with women and this communication garbage, talking about their feelings and expecting you to do the same? There were some things better left unfelt and unsaid. Good luck to her in finding a plumber who wanted to explore his emotions. Or hers. He turned over and buried his head in the pillow.

Once Carrie had a look at the local marriage possibilities, she would realize she was better off in Southern California. Most likely it wouldn't even take the whole week before she realized this place wasn't for her and they'd be heading back to where they belonged. He knew small towns and he wasn't kidding about the gossip. People knew everything before it even happened. And what they didn't know, they made up.

Matt didn't sleep well. It may have been that he was afraid to move, afraid he would roll over to Carrie's side. It may have been his overactive imagination contemplating various scenarios involving Carrie and himself. Or it may have been the quiet. It was so damned quiet out there, except for the pounding of the breakers in the distance. He was used to sleeping with sirens in the background, garbage trucks outside his apartment, and kids yelling. The usual city noises.

When he woke up he saw Carrie on the pillow next to him, her hair a tangled mop of red-gold curls tumbling over her flushed cheek. How many men would have slept next to her all night and not touched her? It was a tribute to his superlative self-control and the respect he had for her.

But now, in the early morning light, he felt some of that self-control slip away. He had a sudden, undeniable urge to kiss her cheek. Just one kiss while she was still asleep. She would never know. He reached out to touch the soft flannel of her sleeve. She stirred and smiled. He wondered who she was dreaming about... the plumber with the sensitive soul or the well digger with the emotional depths that reached to at least two hundred feet.

He inched closer. Were the tips of her eyelashes really gold? Did her freckles continue down onto her chest and farther? He ran his index finger along the curve of her cheek. She sighed deeply and put her arms around him. He held his breath, afraid to move. Then, without a warning, she kissed him, warmly, deeply. Oh, God, if this was a dream, he didn't want to wake up. If it was her dream, let him be a part of it.

She was so sweet, so soft. Her lips parted, and he let his tongue explore the depths as if it were the most natural thing in the world. He pulled her flannel-clad body to him until she melted into him. Her breasts were crushed to his chest, her thighs meshed against his, the gown tangled around her legs, then around his. He held her in his arms, kissing her as if she were his love and not his partner. He forgot about the past, forgot about the future. The way she responded to him, without inhibitions, without hesitation, made him think she'd forgotten, too, and that even while asleep she was just as aroused as he was.

But she hadn't forgotten. When she woke up and realized what was happening, she jerked herself out of his arms and jumped out of bed. She stood there staring at him as if she'd never seen him before. "What happened?" she demanded, running a hand through her glorious copper-colored hair while she gasped for breath.

He shook his head, but couldn't help the half smile that slipped out. "I don't know. I was lying there minding my own business when you turned into a tiger. I didn't know if I'd get out of here alive. But I didn't want to wake you, so I..."

"So you kissed me," she said indignantly.

"Only after you kissed me. You must have been dreaming. Not about me, of course."

"Of course not," she said firmly. Then she frowned. "I can't imagine what possessed me. It must have been the coffee...oh, I didn't have any coffee. Maybe I should have." She looked at the clock on the bedstand. "Oh, Lord, it's late." She rummaged frantically through her suitcase, tossing clothes into piles. "I can't be late, not today. Not my first day."

"Why?" he asked nonchalantly, crossing his arms behind his head.

"Because," she said, feeling the panic rise in her throat, "they're sticklers for promptness. They mentioned on the phone that their last chief was always late...for everything. Would you get up?"

"Of course," he said with an accommodating smile, treating her to another view of his half-naked body as he sprung out from under the sheets. "I wonder where the pancakes are?"

"Pancakes? There's no time for breakfast today." She grabbed her dark suit and her white silk blouse and headed for the bathroom, praying that he would be dressed when she came out. There was just so much a normal woman could take. Why hadn't she brought someone who wore men's flannel pajamas?

Finally, after an eternity of trying to button her blouse with shaking fingers, comb her hair and brush her teeth, she rushed back into the room to find her prayers were answered. Matt was dressed, exactly as a fiancé should be dressed, in tan slacks and a casual, striped, button-down shirt. He looked presentable, personable, decent and, on top of that, unbelievably sexy. Why, oh, why, couldn't he just be presentable? Just for the sake of her peace of mind.

They clattered down the stairs, pausing just long enough to apologize to Mandy for missing breakfast. She wished Carrie good luck and waved to them from the doorway. Before Carrie could open the passenger door of Matt's car, he grabbed her arm.

"Wait a minute," he said. Then he lifted her hair from the back of her neck and tucked the label of her blouse back where it belonged. And slowly, as if they had all the time in the world, he gently kissed the nape of her neck.

Out of the corner of her eye Carrie saw that Mandy was still in the doorway, beaming at them. "I assume that was for her benefit," she said under her breath.

"Of course," he said, opening the door for her.

"Because if it wasn't, I haven't got time for that kind of thing." She pressed her lips together and stared straight ahead while he started the car. The thought of what she'd done that morning haunted her. Had she really come on to him the way he'd said? "We're going to be late," she said, looking at her watch. "Why didn't you wake me up?"

"In the middle of a dream?" He turned onto the two-lane highway they'd left last night. "That's dangerous. You know what Freud said about dreams."

She shook her head and removed the hand-drawn map they'd sent her from her purse.

"A dream is a wish your heart makes," he said solemnly.

She glared at him. "That wasn't Freud, that was Walt Disney. This is no time for jokes. I'm late for the most important appointment of my life, and you're trying to be funny. Can't you drive any faster?"

"What, and get arrested for speeding before you've even taken office? Relax. I'll get you there. You're right. That *was* Disney. I got them mixed up. Freud said dreams are a key to the subconscious mind. So, who *were* you dreaming about?"

"Nobody," she said quickly. Too quickly. Let him guess, let him speculate. He would never know for sure she'd been having the same recurring dreams for months, only this time it had come true. She knew now how it felt to hold him in her arms, to feel the muscles in his chest against the sensitive tips of her breasts. To feel his mouth on hers, to open her lips as if she wanted him to come closer, to delve deeper... She pressed her hand to her head and realized she was holding the map upside down. "Are you sure this is the right way?" she asked as they passed a small airfield on their left.

"Let me see that." He took the map out of her hand. Driving with one hand, he perused the map without missing a beat. "It's back the other way," he announced, swerving to avoid a pothole. "Looks like they could use some money for public works. Maybe you could see about it when you take office."

"I'm going to be the police chief, not the head of the highway department," she informed him.

"What about sending a work crew from the county jail, or do you have a jail right in town?" He turned the car around and drove in the opposite direction.

"I don't know," she said, gripping the edge of the car seat. She was already twenty minutes late and he was going on about the condition of the roads and there was no sign of the town at all, in any direction.

"In one town where I grew up," he continued as if they were out for a Sunday drive with nothing to do but reminisce about his childhood, "the jail was behind the police chief's house. His wife cooked for the prisoners."

"I'd love that."

"Just thought I'd warn you."

"Thanks," she said from between clenched teeth. "Maybe that's why they wanted me to be married. So my husband could do it. Turn here," she said suddenly. "This has to be the road."

Obligingly he turned the steering wheel so abruptly she slid onto his shoulder.

"You sure?" he asked while she straightened and looked at herself in the mirror. She'd meant to do something with her hair, but there'd been no time. Now it stuck out all over her head, and she had a horrible feeling she would never get this job.

"I'm not sure of anything," she admitted, twisting her fingers together in her lap, "except that I'm late, and we're lost."

"We're not lost," he said, coming to a stop when the road dead-ended. "We're just confused." He looked at her, his eyes calm and untroubled as the blue-gray sky overhead. Why should he be troubled? It wasn't his job on the line. She tore her gaze away from his and got out of the car. There on the side of the road was a sign half-hidden by a mulberry bush.

"Lovers Leap," she read out loud. "That's perfect. Maybe I just ought to leap now and save myself the trouble of showing up for the interview an hour late." She drew a ragged breath and got back in the car. "Let's go. We'll ask someone."

"We don't need to ask anyone," he said. "We've got the map."

She bit back a retort, and he kept driving. She was close to tears; she was close to blowing up. But she wasn't close to town. Maybe it just wasn't meant to be. She closed her eyes and when she opened them they were back on a paved road and there were signs to John's Bait Shop and Hansen's Feed and Fuel. Suddenly everything fell into place and in a few more minutes they'd arrived at the civic center, a two-story, white-frame structure that housed the mayor's office, the library and the police headquarters.

"I told you we'd find it," Matt said smugly.

Carrie let herself out of the car, smoothed her skirt and fought the panic that threatened to engulf her. The calmer Matt was, the more she panicked. It was always that way. If he was worried, she maintained her cool, when she lost it, he was calm. It was one of the reasons they were so good together. As partners. Only as partners.

They walked up the steps together and suddenly a group of people appeared, framed in the doorway, anxiously awaiting them.

"I'm Mayor Margaret Thompson," said a motherly looking, gray-haired woman, holding out her hand. "And this is our city council." She introduced them all around. "Ed Harris, Joe Rowley, Lydia Vandermere and Luke Bedford. We've been *waiting* for you. You must be..."

"Carrie Stephens. And this is my..." She couldn't say it, couldn't get the word out. "*Lieutenant* Matt Graham." Matt and Carrie shook hands with the mayor and the council members, which must have taken at least ten minutes. Then the mayor invited them into her office. While Carrie explained why they were late in an aside to the mayor, she overheard one of the councilmen tell Matt he thought he would make a great police chief.

"Thanks, but I'm not..." Matt began.

"Just the kind of guy we're looking for," the man assured him.

"But I'm not interested," Matt said with a glance at Carrie. "It's the lady who's your new police chief."

"What? Maggie," he said in a loud voice to the mayor across the room, "you didn't tell us you'd hired a woman."

"Another woman?" Joe Rowley's face turned purple with anger.

Carrie bit her lip and held on to the side of the mayor's desk.

"What's going on here, Maggie?" demanded Luke Bedford. "You get yourself elected and then you start filling the place with women. First the sanitation engineer who didn't know squat about sanitation and now her." He jerked his head in Carrie's direction. "Is she even qualified?"

"Now wait just a darn minute," the mayor said with an authority that belied her grandmotherly appearance. "It happens that *Lieutenant* Stephens here is perfectly qualified for the job. The *most* qualified of all two hundred applicants. I circulated her application. Nobody objected. You all agreed."

"But you didn't tell us. . ."

"You never said . . ."

"You lied . . ."

"I never lied. I never said she was a woman because it has nothing to do with the job. May I remind you who read her curriculum vitae, that she's been decorated for bravery, has a degree in public administration, served for ten years in the Los Angeles police department during which she was . . ." The mayor reached for her bifocals and Carrie's résumé from her desk.

"Named Rookie of the Year and won the Medal of Honor," Matt interjected.

Carrie smiled weakly. The rest of them stared at Matt.

"Who're you?" Luke asked. At least, Carrie thought it was Luke. They were all starting to blend together.

"Police Lieutenant Matt Graham," he said.

"What's wrong with him? Why can't we have *him* for our police chief?" Lydia Vandermere demanded with an admiring glance at Matt.

Et tu, Carrie thought. Even the one woman on the council wanted a man for the job.

"I'm just here with my..." he seemed to trip over the word, too. "My...fiancée. I'm not interested in the job."

"Why not? What are you going to do, let your wife wear the pants in the family?" Luke demanded.

"Long as she doesn't wear them to bed at night," Matt said with a gleam in his eye.

Carrie felt her face turn scarlet as all eyes focused on her. How dare he make such a sexist remark? How dare he treat her like a sex object? The room fell silent. She wished she could crawl under the desk. The whole world was against her. Except for the mayor. *She* wanted her for the job. Maybe together they could convince the others. But it didn't look good.

"Thank you for bringing Lt. Stephens to us, Lt. Graham," the mayor said, breaking the silence and taking Matt by the arm to show him to the door. "We'll be seeing you later, tonight at the potluck supper. You'll get to meet the whole town then. Won't that be fun?" she asked with a twinkle in her eye.

"Can hardly wait," Matt drawled. Then, under his breath, he said, "Carrie can do everything I can do except get places on time. So don't let those bozos push you around, Mayor."

"I won't," she assured with a confidential wink. "Especially since one of them is my husband."

Matt managed a smile then stumbled down the front steps feeling like a jerk for undercutting Carrie like that. First making her late, then for his remark to the mayor. He was torn. Did he or didn't he want her to get this job? He wanted the best for her—that he knew for sure. And the best was returning with him to L.A. to be his partner.

They'd had two good years and they would have many more as soon as she realized that this wasn't the place for her. And since she hadn't realized it yet, he would have to make sure the town realized it.

But Matt hoped he wouldn't have to do any more sabotaging. He headed toward Main Street with the goal of finding the local equivalent of Victoria's Secret, unwilling to analyze his motives for continuing to throw himself into the fiancé game. The only thing he was up to analyzing this morning was how different Carrie would feel in silk and lace tonight.

"I should have told them it was my fault you were late this morning," Matt said when he picked Carrie up at five o'clock that evening. And he meant it when he said it. Because his heart twisted when he saw how down and out she looked, with her eyes glazed and her face pale. He wanted to pick her up and carry her back to bed to recuperate and carry on where they'd left off that morning. But there was that damned potluck dinner ahead of them. And there was no going back. Uncharted territory lay ahead of them, and he wasn't sure from moment to moment what his position was.

Matt wanted to ask Carrie how things went, but he didn't. He wanted to know if she'd had enough yet of small towns, if she was ready to go home, but he didn't dare ask. All he could do was hope she would make the right decision without any more "help" from him. Or that the town would make the decision for her. Had they done it already? Is that what was wrong with her?

"Hey," he said softly after he'd opened the car door for her and climbed back into the driver's seat. "Are you all right?"

She nodded and turned her head in his direction. "It wasn't easy," she said, "but I think I've got the job."

He felt like he'd been slammed in the ribs with a riot baton. He didn't think it would happen so soon. He wasn't quite ready to congratulate her. But she was looking at him. Waiting for him to say something.

"That's great," he said. "Then I can go home." Go home alone. Without her. Without Carrie. His partner.

Her face paled. She gripped his arm. "No, you can't. They're making plans for us. Wedding plans."

Chapter Four

"Wedding plans? Wait a minute, a wedding was not part of the deal." Matt turned the key in the ignition and the car leapt forward.

Carrie pressed her lips together to keep them from trembling. All day she'd answered questions about her past, present and future. About what she would do in a hostage situation at the grade school, or an armed robbery at the farmer's market or even an invasion of refugee fishing boats until her brain had turned to mush. And then they'd sprung the wedding thing on her. She didn't need Matt to remind her how distasteful he found the whole idea. He looked like she'd suggested head-hunting in New Guinea. But, she realized, even that might be more appealing to him than marrying her.

"Don't worry," she assured him as he drove through town with his brow furrowed and his eyes staring straight ahead. "It won't be necessary to go that far."

"It better not be. Because one wedding is enough for most people. And one too many for this cop. Cops should never get married in the first place."

"What should they do, take a vow of celibacy?" she asked, surprised at the intensity in his voice. "It seems to me cops need support on the home front even more than other people do." Keep it impersonal, she told herself, don't even try to pry any information out of him, because he'll clam up as tight as one of those mollusk on the beach.

"That's where you're wrong," he advised her, hunching over the steering wheel. "If you'd ever been married you'd know what I mean. It's impossible to give it your all both at home and at work. So you have to make a choice."

Carrie stole a glance at Matt's profile, at the slight bump in his nose from broken cartilage, at the small scar in his chin from a cut from a fight.

"And you chose your work," she suggested.

"You got it. Or I'd still be married."

"It's as simple as that?"

"Marriage isn't simple at all. It took me three years to figure it out. By then it was too late. She'd left."

Touched by the sadness she read between the lines, Carrie reached out and put her hand on his arm. "Maybe it wasn't your fault."

He shot her an impatient look. "It wasn't anybody's fault."

"Then you don't have any reason to feel guilty."

"I don't," he said. "But I learned a valuable lesson. Stay away from relationships."

Carrie dropped her hand from his arm. She knew what that meant. Stay away from women who make demands, who want a commitment. He drove slowly down Main Street and brought the subject back to the wedding. Anything so he wouldn't have to talk about himself.

"So, tell me more about this wedding that's not going to happen," he said.

Carrie sighed and looked out the window at the small shops that lined the street. "All right. I didn't know it, but this fall the town is celebrating its one hundred and fiftieth birthday. They've spent the last year raising money to restore the first house ever built, the historic Delarosa House, and refurnish it to the way it was during the Spanish land grant days. So along with the opening of the house as a museum, they're going to throw a wedding for us. They'll provide us with authentic clothes, invite the newspapers, the historical society and...well, you get the picture."

"I get the picture. They're using you—us to promote the town. I can see it now in the Moss Beach *Gazette*..."

"*Courier,*" she corrected.

"*Courier.* Police Chief Weds In Historic House. 'When asked about his plans, her husband confessed he didn't have a clue. He's just along for the ride, he said.'"

"What's wrong with that?" Carrie asked, scarcely noticing that he'd driven to the public beach and parked in the lot on the bluffs above the ocean. "So far it hasn't been a bad ride, has it?"

Matt got out of the car without answering her, and Carrie wished she hadn't mentioned the wedding. It was bound to upset him. But if she hadn't told him, someone else would have. She opened the car door and joined him on the cliff, letting the stiff breeze blow through her hair and cool her cheeks. She couldn't pretend his attitude didn't hurt, or that his reaction to marrying her didn't chill her more than the air off the ocean, she just couldn't let it show.

"It's a good ride," he said at last. "So far. But you caught me off guard with that wedding stuff."

"I know," she said. "But I figure we just go along with it, agree to whatever they want, the wedding, the costumes, the publicity until after you leave. I'll break the news that you've had second thoughts, changed your mind and broke our engagement."

He slanted a look at her with eyes that matched the gray of the sea and sky. "You'll be heartbroken, of course," he suggested.

She studied his face, the familiar lines that forked out from the corners of his eyes, the slightly crooked nose and the stubborn chin, and she knew that if anyone could break her heart it would be him. But she managed a half smile. "Not too heartbroken, I hope. After all, I'm a professional, and I wouldn't let it interfere with my work. But I'll be disappointed, almost as disappointed as they are, of course."

"Of course," he said, matching her attempt at a smile with one of his own. "Do we have time to walk on the beach?"

She looked at her watch and nodded.

He looked down at her stockinged feet and high-heeled shoes. "Leave those in the car," he instructed.

She peeled off her shoes and stockings and set them on top of a rock. "They'll be all right here," she said.

"Are you sure?"

"Of course I'm sure. This is Moss Beach, not West L.A. This is the whole reason I'm moving here. Look around. Do you see any graffiti, any beer cans, hear any gunfire?"

He shrugged. "They're your shoes."

"That's right. The only good shoes I brought with me. That's how sure I am."

They clambered down the steep trail to the beach, Carrie so hampered by her narrow skirt that Matt had to turn and lift her by the waist and set her down on the wet sand at the bottom. For a brief moment he paused, his hands still on her hips, and looked down at her. "Why don't *you* break our engagement?" he asked. "Why do I have to be the bad guy?"

Carrie stared at him, taken aback by his question. Just for a moment it seemed like a real engagement they were discussing. Standing there on the beach with the waves crashing against the shore, the pressure from his hand sending spirals of sensation down, down...into the depths of her being, it almost seemed possible that he might be in love with her, so in love, they were engaged.

She told herself it wasn't possible. If he hadn't fallen for her in the last two years, when they'd spent every waking minute together, then it wasn't going to happen.

"Me break our engagement?" she asked at last. "Why would I do that?"

"You could say I'm difficult, strong-willed, opinionated, stubborn..."

"Domineering and skeptical," she added enthusiastically.

"See, it's not hard." He took her hand and they walked along the shore.

"But they'll say, 'Then why did you get engaged in the first place?'"

"And you'll say..." he prompted, lifting a strand of hair from her forehead and tucking it behind her ear.

She shivered. Just the touch of his hand, just a look in his eyes, made her heart flutter so she couldn't think. "I'll say, uh, I didn't really know him, not until we came to Moss Beach." That part was true. She had the feeling he was changing before her very eyes. Whether for the better or the worse, she didn't know. She just knew he was different. There was something in his gaze she'd never seen before, an awareness that hadn't been there before. She tore her eyes away, afraid he would see too much and guess the truth. The last thing in the world she wanted from him was his sympathy. "I guess it's time to go," she said.

"Race you back to the car," he said, taking off without her.

"No fair," she yelled at him. "I'm wearing a skirt."

"Take it off," he shouted over his shoulder.

She shook her head and walked slowly down the beach behind him. This lighthearted side of Matt Graham was due to his willingness to play the game and to pose as her fiancé. She knew that, but she didn't know why he carried it over into their private moments, like just now, when there was no need. No need at all.

Carrie arrived at the top of the trail panting and out of breath. Her shoes were not on the rock where she'd left them. She walked to the car and opened the door on the driver's side. "Give me my shoes," she said to Matt, who was studying a map of the area he'd picked up in town that day.

"Don't have them."

"They're gone."

"They can't be gone. There's no crime in Moss Beach," he said smugly.

"At least there wasn't until we came here. Come on, you've made your point. Give them back to me."

"I don't have them," he insisted. "Have we got time to go back and get another pair from the inn?" he asked without looking up from his map.

"No, we don't," she snapped. His calm in the midst of this crisis was beginning to annoy her. That and the feeling he enjoyed seeing her proved wrong.

"I've got some sandals in the trunk," he offered.

She stared at him in disbelief. As if he didn't know his shoes would be miles too big for her. She continued staring until he looked up.

"Want me to get them for you?" he asked.

"If you're sure you don't mind," she said sarcastically.

The shoes were ridiculous. She felt like Donald Duck when she took a few experimental steps, but they were better than going barefoot to her first social function in town. Matt told her they looked fine, but his lips twitched with the hint of a smile as he got back into the car.

"Are you sure you didn't see any suspicious characters hanging around?" she asked on the way back to town.

He gave her a sharp glance. "Why don't you put out an all-points bulletin? You want to establish yourself as tough on crime from the beginning."

"Very funny."

"Come on, Carrie. It was probably some kids playing a prank. Forget it."

"That's easy for you to say. Don't you realize I'm being watched, scrutinized and tested every minute during these next two weeks? From what I wear to what I do and say? This was no prank. This was part of a plot to sabotage me and my job."

Matt gave her a look that said it all. That he thought she'd gone over the edge into paranoia. Maybe she had. Maybe the pressure was getting to her. Of trying to look good to the town, of trying to look engaged. "Never mind. You're right. It was just some kids playing a prank. I don't need those shoes anyway. I brought another pair." Unfortunately they were her running shoes. And they didn't go with dress-for-success suits.

He nodded approvingly. "Good girl."

The potluck dinner was held in the multipurpose room at the high school. Carrie met so many people her head was swimming. And when they noticed her shoes, she told them high heels threw her off balance and prevented her from chasing down thieves. They seemed so impressed she even told a few people who *didn't* notice her lack of appropriate footwear.

She hadn't spoken to Matt since they'd walked in the front door, but she caught an occasional glimpse of him across the crowded gym floor. He was always surrounded by an admiring group of people hanging on his every word. It wasn't surprising. He was so good-looking, had so much confidence that oozed from every pore, such mental and physical toughness that if she'd just met him, she would probably be hanging on every word, too.

That's why it wasn't going to be believable to tell people she'd broken up with him. They would never understand why. She tore her eyes from his tall, muscular frame and concentrated on the people sitting at her dinner table.

Over plates heaped high with generous servings of lasagna and giant slices of garlic bread, they asked Carrie what she was going to do about the litter on the beaches and drugs in the schools.

Startled, she said she wasn't aware of litter or drugs. It turned out they just wanted to prevent these problems. Carrie told them about her successful drug prevention program in the L.A. schools and convinced them that if they stayed vigilant they could keep crime out of Moss Beach. Reassured, they beamed at her, and never once did anyone ask about her fiancé. Her fiancé, who now was joining the mayor at the coffeemaker at the end of the buffet table. The mayor poured him a cup of coffee and Carrie winced.

Matt was a fanatic about coffee. Bought his beans freshly roasted from a certain place on La Cienega and ground them himself. Potluck dinner coffee made in thirty-cup quantities hours ahead of time would never make the grade.

The mayor gave Matt a warm smile. Carrie wished she knew what they were talking about.

"I've had nothing but good reports about your fiancée," Mayor Thompson confided to Matt in a low, confidential tone. "She's made a big hit tonight and today at the interviews."

"Then there's no real reason she shouldn't get the job?" Matt asked, adding cream to the dark brown brew.

"She showed our council that she would be just as tough on crime as any man, which solves the gender issue," said the mayor. "Of course, some people were upset when she arrived late, but given she didn't know the way, first day and all, well, I'm sure it won't happen again."

Matt nodded. Not unless the alarm didn't go off or she got distracted. The idea of a distraction like the one that happened that morning brought a smile to his lips. The memory of those kisses had haunted him all day.

"And the shoes," the mayor continued. "I notice she's not a slave to fashion. She has the confidence to dress for the job, and up here we like that."

"Up here and everywhere," Matt said, seeking out Carrie's face in the crowd.

"But there is one thing..." Mayor Thompson hesitated. "There are some folks who are worried about you."

Matt sloshed his coffee over the rim of his cup. "Me?"

"What are you going to do here?" she asked, her blue eyes fixed on him intently.

"Carrie wants me to retire," he said, catching Carrie's eye across the room.

"Are you ready to hang up your uniform?" she inquired.

"She comes first," Matt continued. He thought it sounded good, like something he should say. But he didn't mean it. Because nobody came first with him, just himself. That's why his first marriage had failed. Because he put himself and his job first. Because he watched his marriage fall apart and didn't do anything to save it. He wasn't capable of the kind of selflessness it took to make a marriage work. He looked up. Carrie smiled at him from across the room, a warm, reassuring smile as if she knew what he was thinking. But the mayor didn't.

She would find out soon enough. When he left, and Carrie had to explain what happened. Then she could tell everyone what a self-centered jerk he was and would continue to be. Despite what he'd said to Carrie, he didn't mind taking the blame for their failed engagement. But maybe it wouldn't come to that. He still had hopes she would come to her senses and go back with him. Then nobody would have to be the bad guy. And life could go on as it was. As it should. With them as partners. Back on the beat. Because without her... The thought of life without her gave him an empty feeling.

The mayor gave Matt a long, hard look, then she smiled with satisfaction. "That's what I wanted to hear," she said. "That Carrie comes first. I think the chief of police needs some solid support when she comes home at night. Not that you won't want *something* to do, something meaningful. By the way, have you seen the house yet?"

"No...no, we haven't." Damn. He'd forgotten all about the house that went with the job. Once Carrie saw the house, if it was even halfway decent, she would never leave. She would be here and he would be there, six hundred miles away.

He glanced across the room and saw Carrie still answering questions from eager citizens. He saw her rub her forehead with one hand. Her eyes were drooping at half-mast. If he were really her fiancé, he would smooth away her fatigue with his hands. He would insist on taking her home immediately. When they got there he would kiss her until she forgot she was tired. She would look over at him, as she was doing now, and he would know her innermost thoughts. Know that she wanted him, needed him...

"Excuse me, Your Honor," he said. Crossing the room, he took Carrie by the arm and told her it was time to go.

She gave him a grateful smile and said goodbye. As they walked outside, he said, "You looked tired."

In the car she rested her head against the seat back. "What a day. *Getting* this job has got to be harder than *doing* this job."

"I wouldn't count on it," he warned. "I spotted several potential criminals in that crowd, including myself. I'd like to kill the person who brewed that coffee. What do they use around here, 150-year-old beans?"

"Maybe gourmet coffee isn't high on their list of priorities."

"Obviously not. And you still want to work here?"

"Yes," she assured him. "What were you and the mayor talking about?"

"You."

Carrie's forehead puckered into a frown. "She doesn't suspect, does she?"

"That neither of us has any intention of getting married? I don't think so. But she wanted to know what I'm going to do when we move here. So I told her I might retire."

"There must be something you could do," she mused.

"Like what. Whittling? Stamp collecting? I don't have any hobbies. All I know is my work." He pulled up in front of the bed and breakfast and turned off the ignition. She knew she should go in, but instead she stayed.

"Yes, yes, I know," she said. But she'd forgotten. She actually thought it was real, the need to find a new job for Matt. A sudden shaft of sadness pierced her heart. It was all a ruse, a hoax, a plot to fool the town. But instead it had almost fooled her.

"Don't move," Matt cautioned in a low voice. "Somebody's watching us from the front room. Probably wondering what we're doing out here so late at night." He exhaled slowly. "I guess we'll have to show them."

"What—"

Before she could formulate her question, he answered it with a kiss. A kiss so unexpected and so earthshaking she couldn't think, couldn't breathe, couldn't do anything but let herself give in to the sensations racing through her veins. Talk about forgetting. Talk about reality blending with make-believe. She no longer knew where one ended and the other began. And she didn't care.

The only thing she cared about was Matt. And she could have sworn he cared about her, too. The way his mouth molded to hers, the way his hands cupped her face and steadied her while his mouth sought hers. She kicked off his oversize sandals and twisted on the seat to return his kisses, which increased in intensity.

The fatigue of an hour ago was gone. Instead she was burning with a new energy she'd never known she had. Her hands moved to his face, then downward, her palms flat against the rigid muscles of his chest. He groaned and the kisses went on, stronger and more intense. His arms tightened around her until his back was pressed against the door. He was stroking her back, reaching down until his hands cupped her bottom. In another few minutes they would be flat on the seat, tearing off each other's clothes.

Why? she wondered, when they had that big bed in there, that big soft bed ... With a gasp, Carrie pulled away from Matt. The bed. How could she have forgotten this meant nothing to him? That he was doing it for show and that they faced another awkward night sleeping in the same bed?

She reached for her shoes. "That ought to convince them," she said, bending over to buckle the sandals. She didn't look at him, but she knew how he would look. Calm, poised, and completely in control. He had the remarkable ability to turn his ardor off and on for her benefit. All to help her get her job. She wanted to think she would do the same for him. But she knew she couldn't. She would never be able to walk out of his life after two weeks with him. It had only been two days and look at her. She reached for the car door and stumbled out into the cool fresh air.

There was no one at the window now, no one in the doorway to welcome them. She waited for him to join her at the door, then shot him an inquiring look.

"Looks like everyone's gone to bed," he said, reaching for the door handle. He was so calm, so steady. She wasn't surprised. That's the way he'd always been. What made him so good at his job. Was this the same man who'd kissed her a few minutes ago, as if he couldn't stop, wouldn't stop, unless she did? She could have sworn he wanted her, was close to doing something about it, but that couldn't be.

She looked around at the empty living room, at the comfortable chairs that welcomed the guests. "Whoever it was," she said, "we showed them."

Matt didn't answer. Instead he turned back to the door. "You go on up, I left something in the car."

Carrie nodded, removed his sandals and dragging her feet, walked slowly up the stairs, too tired to think, emotionally and physically spent.

Walking past the bed without looking at it, she went straight to the bathroom to brush her teeth and retrieve the nightgown she'd left hanging on the hook that morning. It wasn't there. There were neat stacks of fresh towels, scented soap and complimentary shampoo. But no nightgown.

First her shoes, now her nightgown. She was losing everything. So much for her plan to be in bed before Matt arrived. But already she heard his footsteps on the stairs. She sat on the edge of the bed, propped her head in her hands and waited.

Matt opened the door with one hand behind his back. "Close your eyes," he said.

Her eyelids fluttered closed. He thrust a cardboard box into her hands. With her eyes still closed, she lifted the lid. The tips of her fingers brushed against fabric so soft and silky it must have been woven by the gods.

"You can open them now." Matt's voice reminded her of rough sandpaper.

"I'm afraid to. What is it?"

"It's your new nightgown."

Her eyes flew open. He was standing next to the bed looking down at her. "What a coincidence. My old nightgown disappears and a new one appears."

"I told you the other one wasn't right for your pre-honeymoon."

"So you took it."

He shook his head. "Maybe Mandy put it in the laundry. Anything else missing?"

Only the sense she was born with. Only her self-control. Other than that... "I don't know. I can't seem to think very well." She took the nightgown out of the box and went into the bathroom.

Matt stood staring at the closed door. He hadn't expected her to jump for joy at the sight of the sexiest gown ever sold in Moss Beach, but a thank-you would have been nice, or even a kiss. Talk about kisses. Where had all that pent-up passion come from? Was that really his cool, calm and collected partner back there in the car?

Sure, he'd started it with the story that someone was watching them, someone who needed to be convinced their involvement was for real. The real story was, he couldn't stop himself. All evening he'd been watching her mingle, making small talk with strangers, when she was supposed to be with him, her fiancé. Not really, of course, but somewhere along the line the story had gotten confused with reality in his mind. It must have been that godawful coffee that did it. Because in the car, sitting so close to her, inhaling the scent of almond and honey, he'd had to kiss her. He'd had to find out, before it was too late, what it would be like.

And she'd responded like someone who'd been trapped behind a bulletproof vest for too long. He paced back and forth in front of the window replaying the scene, the way she'd pinned him against the door with her hands on his chest, her mouth meeting his. With every minute that passed, his heart rate increased, his anticipation doubled, tripled as he imagined how she'd look in that nightgown, what they'd do in bed when she came out.

"Where did you get this?" Her voice drifted out the door.

"At a store on Main Street. Why, doesn't it fit?"

"I'm not sure. It's a little low in front, a little... I don't know how it's supposed to be."

"Want me to take it back?" he said under his breath.

"Then I'd have nothing to wear."

"Uh-huh."

Silence. Had she heard him? Would she ever come out of there?

She came out. The pale green satin flowed from the décolletage between her breasts to her ankles, caressing the curve of her hip the way he would like to. Her red-gold hair brushed against her bare shoulders with the sheen of polished copper. He didn't realize he was holding his breath until she spoke.

"I suppose I ought to thank you." Her cheeks were flushed, but her dark brown gaze didn't waver from his. Did she know how utterly desirable she was in that pale green foam that appeared to have been sprayed onto her?

He shrugged with an effort to be casual. In another minute he would be drooling like a Saint Bernard. "That's not necessary. It's just what any fiancé would have done. Under the circumstances. The romantic B and B, the bridal suite... all that." He couldn't stop, couldn't keep his eyes off the way the silk fabric shimmered and glimmered in the lamplight. "I'm just glad it fits," he continued, babbling like an idiot. Why didn't he just shut up and go into the bathroom?

There was just so much stimulation a man could take. He was there as Carrie's stand-in fiancé. She didn't want a real one and neither did he. There were times when it was hard to remember that. Like now. He stumbled into the shower and stood there until the hot water ran out and then he stood there for another ten minutes. Maybe Carrie would be asleep when he got out. He sincerely hoped so, because if she was still standing there like a siren rising out of the mist, he would have to tie himself to the bedpost.

But there was no reason to worry. She was fast asleep on her side of the bed. The only light came from the night-light near the door. He breathed a huge sigh of relief. This situation would never have happened if they'd only stayed where they'd belonged. As soon as they went back, things would be back to normal. He had to believe that. If he didn't, he might be worried. Worried that he couldn't forget how she looked in pale green silk or how she felt in his arms in this bed or how she tasted in the dark interior of his car. It was this place. This house. This town. This damned sea air. That's all. It was doing strange things to him. To her, too.

He slid between the sheets, acutely aware of Carrie on the far side of the bed, her sweet scent wafting his way. How many more nights would he have to endure this torture? How long would it take her to realize this was not the place for her? Was it wrong to help her come to that conclusion?

He couldn't fall asleep right away. Maybe because he had second thoughts about what he was doing. He had to remember that he was doing it for her own good. That one day she might even thank him for it. Not today or tomorrow. Maybe around the time of her twenty-fifth year with the L.A.P.D., the year she got her gold watch. She would look at him and say thank-you. Yes, that would be the day.

Carrie never thought she would sleep at all, dressed like someone out of a lingerie catalog. She was the flannel type, the buttons-up-to-the-chin type. Always had been, always would be. And yet the touch of satin against her skin, the smooth, cool caress of the gown, sent her off into dreamland as soon as her head hit the pillow. Granted, her dreams were erotic in nature, prominently featuring the man who was her partner, her phony fiancé, the man who slept next to her with one arm thrown across his pillow. Slowly and very carefully she turned on her side to look at him. Knowing he was asleep, taking advantage of the situation to take a good, long look in the pale, early morning light.

The lines in his forehead were gone. The taut muscles around his mouth had relaxed. He looked younger, happier than she'd ever seen him. If only he could always be that much at peace with himself and with the world. It was this place, this town, this house and this vacation. If only she could make it last.

He could quit his job and come to Moss Beach like she was doing. He didn't have to marry her to do it. He wouldn't do that. He'd tried marriage and it didn't work. Maybe if she'd tried it once, she would be disillusioned, too. But she hadn't and she wasn't. His dark hair fell across his forehead. She wanted to reach out and smooth it back.

Her alarm went off, and he buried his head under his pillow. She jumped out of bed and took the suit off the hanger she'd hung in the closet. "You don't have to get up," she whispered to the shapeless form under the comforter. "I can get myself to town if I take your car."

"Mumph."

"Is that a yes?"

He didn't answer. She tiptoed into the bathroom, took a shower and dressed in a gray suit and a red-and-gray paisley blouse with a huge floppy bow she'd bought especially for this trip. For years she'd lived in uniforms or shorts and T-shirts. Nothing in between. Now all of a sudden she was expected to look like a job applicant. With her suit she'd planned to wear her Italian leather pumps, the ones she'd left on the rock, instead she would show up today in scuffed running shoes. At least they fit better than Matt's sandals. She laced them up and looked in the full-length mirror. From the ankles up she could pass for anybody—doctor, lawyer, merchant or...chief of police.

She paused at the bedroom door and looked back at Matt. "Bye," she said softly.

He squinted up at her and smiled sleepily. "You look great. How about I come to town and we do lunch?"

"*Do* lunch...in Moss Beach? How would you get there?"

"Catch a ride from someone at the inn."

She stood there watching him, wanting nothing more than to get back into bed, feel his arms around her, his warm body— Good heavens, what was wrong with her?

A slow sleepy smile crossed his face as if he knew what she was thinking. "How about a goodbye kiss?" he asked.

She gripped the doorknob. The memory of his lips on hers, of the hunger that drew her to him came back with a rush. "Why?" she asked lightly. "There's no one around. No one to impress."

He propped himself on his elbow. "It just seemed like the thing to do. A man's fiancée goes off on a job interview. He deserves a kiss. Maybe more."

The look in his eyes told her how much more he wanted, and she felt a flush creep up her neck. Sometimes she wondered if she'd ever known this man at all. In all the years she'd known him she'd never seen this side of him. She'd dreamed of him turning into a warm, outgoing kind of guy. But here her dreams had come true beyond her wildest imagination. It was disturbing, unsettling. As if Clark Kent and Superman had blended into one with an extra helping of sexual chemistry sizzling between them.

He was looking at her, waiting for her. She walked silently to the side of the bed in her rubber-tread shoes, leaned down and kissed him briefly on the cheek. Then she left quickly without looking back. Before she could change her mind, before she could wonder what might have happened if she'd stayed. She knew one thing. If she was late again, she would be in trouble.

And she wouldn't have been late if it hadn't been for the flat tire. And she wouldn't have had a flat tire if it hadn't been for the potholes on the dirt road outside of town. Carrie didn't waste any time standing next to the car waiting for someone to come along. She took off in her running shoes and walked all the way into town, arriving a good three-quarters of an hour late.

She apologized to the council. They exchanged pointed looks, then they rushed off to take her on a tour of the breakwater, the fishing fleet and the so-called yacht harbor. On the pier she found a public phone and called Matt to tell him about the flat tire.

"I had to leave the car. I'm sorry, but the road's so rough there."

"I know. I'll take care of it. Are you still free for lunch?"

"Oh, no, I don't think so." It was bad enough spending evenings and nights with him, lunch was out of the question.

"Made any headway solving the mystery of the missing shoes?"

She bit her lip. "Not yet. But I think I've got it narrowed down."

"Good for you."

Carrie tried to make up for being late by suggesting ways to check on fishermen surpassing the limits and for improving safety on the vessels. The mayor nodded; her husband, who was in charge of public works and safety, took notes. By the time they got back to the office Carrie was feeling pretty good.

Until the mayor mentioned the wedding again. "We'd like to have a practice run," she said, "with you and your future husband in costume. That way we can get some good publicity shots to promote the celebration."

Carrie looked out the window of the mayor's office at the town square. She could just see Matt in suspenders across his chest and a high, starched collar that scratched his stubborn chin. That might push him over the edge and send him home before the probation period was over.

"It's just that we're so busy right now," Carrie protested gently.

The mayor nodded her gray head. "Aren't we all," she agreed. "The historical society is working night and day on this. Everything is going to be completely authentic."

Except for the groom, Carrie thought.

"There's your man now," the mayor said, going to the window. "How I envy you. I just wish my Luke looked at me the way he looks at you. Just remember, things change as you grow old. Enjoy it while you can."

Carrie smiled wanly and went out the front door to meet Matt before the mayor scared him with the publicity plans. But before they got beyond the sidewalk, the mayor came bustling out to give them the key to their new house.

"I can't believe you haven't seen it yet. I meant to take you there the first day. But it's better this way. Just the two of you alone together." She pursed her lips as if she could hardly stand the thrill they were going to experience in just a few minutes. "It's right around the corner, walking distance to work. Behind the nursery."

"Nursery?" Carrie inquired.

"Nursery... for plants. Oh, you thought I meant for children." The mayor chuckled. "No, not yet." She gave them a knowing smile and went back to work.

Carrie paled. First an engagement, then a wedding rehearsal in full regalia, and now a baby. What more could they ask of her?

Chapter Five

Matt and Carrie walked in silence past renovated houses that included a dentist's office as well as a yogurt shop, all with flower boxes out in front.

"I was wondering when that would come up," Carrie mused.

"What?"

"The nursery. The question of pregnancy. Employers always ask women, which is really unfair in this case since they're the ones insisting I be married."

"They haven't asked you, have they?" Matt said.

"Not yet. But I'll bet you anything the council would object if I had a baby."

Startled, he asked, "Do you *want* to have a baby?"

"Not if I'm not married." They turned the corner.

He slanted a look at her out of the corner of his eye. "And if you were?"

She shook her head. "Can you see me making the rounds with a baby in a stroller and a backpack?" She stared off into space, a strange preoccupied look in her eyes.

Strangely enough he *could* see it. Carrie pushing a red-haired baby up and down Main Street, greeting townspeople like the friendly neighborhood cop she was. But when he thought of the baby in the line of fire, even though there was no fire in Moss Beach, he shook his head. "Better leave her in daycare." Her? Where had that come from?

"I guess. Although, if they ask, I could say I'll leave her at home."

"But you'll be at work," he noted.

"You won't."

"Wait a minute." He stopped abruptly and gripped her arm. "*I'm* supposed to take care of this baby?"

"You were wondering what to do with yourself. Anyway, it's not real. It's all hypothetical."

"I'm not taking care of any baby, real *or* hypothetical," he assured her.

"I know that and you know that. But they don't have to know that. It would answer both of their major concerns, what's the police chief's husband going to do and what if the police chief gets pregnant? I realize it's an imposition."

"An imposition?" He dropped her arm but held her with his gaze. "I don't know anything about it, but I assume a baby is a hell of a lot more than an imposition."

She rocked back on the heels of her sneakers. "Don't worry about it. It will never come to that. I just want to be prepared for whatever they throw at me. I'm not going to let this job slip through my fingers because of a technicality."

"You call a baby a technicality?" he asked.

She gave an exasperated sigh. "You know what I mean." For a long moment they stood in front of the plant nursery, and looked at each other. Was she asking too much of him? Carrie wondered. It wasn't as if she really expected a man who'd never missed a day of work in his life to suddenly turn into Mr. Mom. But here they were discussing a nonexistent baby as if it were real or at least a possibility. Which it wasn't.

"Let's go see the house," she said, realizing that he hadn't said yes and he hadn't said no. He was just going to leave her hanging, hoping that the questions she feared would never come up.

Matt was afraid to look at the house. Even more afraid to look at Carrie looking at the house. He was aware of her reactions, though. He heard her suck in her breath at the sight of the gables on the roof and the fresh white paint and the chocolate brown trim. He saw her hand caress the polished brass front doorknob and heard her sigh with pleasure before she'd even opened the door.

He did everything he could to discourage her. Looked for termite damage, for dry rot, for a sagging foundation. But she wasn't worried. "Termites I can handle. Now spiders are a different matter."

"As if I didn't know," he said. "As if I could forget that night in a dark alley when we were picking up a drunk for vagrancy and you thought you saw a spider..."

"I *did* see one." She shuddered at the recollection. "But did I let it interfere with my job?"

"Not if you think letting out an ear-splitting scream that woke the entire neighborhood was part of your job."

"I'm better now," she assured him. "I use self-hypnosis."

"Good, because I won't always be around to lift you down from a convenient garbage container."

She nodded. "I know that."

He'd hoped she would say, "Then I'd better stick with you, go back where you'll always *be* around." But she didn't. So he continued to run down the house by commenting on the lack of space in the one-car garage, on the condition of the roof and a missing tile in the bathroom, but she just ignored him as she went from room to room, admiring every square foot of carpet as she went. She finally paused in the master bedroom on the second floor, flung open the window and gazed down into the backyard.

"Did you ever live in a house like this?" she asked.

"Many houses, but none like this," he admitted. Okay, so the house had a certain charm.

"You moved around a lot?" she asked, still looking down at the brick patio and the clipped grass around it.

"Yeah."

"My family never had a house," she said wistfully.

"Mine didn't, either," he said. "These were foster homes."

She looked at him with surprise. "I didn't know that."

"It's not something I talk about." He hadn't planned on talking about it today, either. He didn't know why he was.

"Was it awful?" she asked softly.

He wished she wouldn't look at him like that, with her dark eyes brimming with sympathy. "It was worse for the people who took me in. I wasn't easy to handle. The kind of kid who ends up in jail or being a cop. I was lucky it turned out this way. The kids I hung out with went the other way."

"But how—"

"What about you?" he cut in. "Have you lived in apartments all your life?"

She nodded. "They were always saving to buy a house, but they split up before it happened. Now I'm saving, but it would take me another twenty years before I had enough to buy a place in L.A. and then it would be a fixer-upper or a handyman special. So you can see how much this means, to be handed this house. I know it wouldn't really be mine, not right away, but it comes with an option to buy." She inhaled the scent of the roses that grew along the edge of the house. "Anyway, it feels like mine," she said with a smile.

It gave Matt a weird feeling in the pit of his stomach to watch her fall in love with this house. To hear how much it meant to her. He felt helpless to stop her, and he was afraid she would never go back with him now, no matter what happened.

No matter how narrow-minded the people were or how dull the job was. No matter how many pairs of shoes were stolen. He studied her face with the sunlight turning her freckles to flecks of gold, her hair escaping from the knot she'd twisted it into that morning, and he knew he'd have to take bold measures to make her or the town change their mind. And he'd better do it fast.

"How about lunch?" he asked in an effort to put some distance between them and the house.

"I think I'll just stay here," she said, gazing down at the hammock stretched between two apple trees, at the white lattice gazebo and the wrought-iron table and chairs on the patio.

Matt frowned. He might as well not even be here for all she cared. She was using him to get the job and the house. As soon as she had them sewed up, then she would discard him like a disposable cigarette lighter. He knew it. He'd known it since the beginning. She hadn't even *asked* him to come, he reminded himself. He'd offered. "I'll go pick up some sandwiches from the deli and bring them back," he offered.

She nodded absently. "I'll be downstairs in the garden."

When Matt came back with the food, Carrie was stretched out in the hammock with her eyes closed and a blissful smile on her face. He paused at the edge of the grass and looked at her. She's in paradise, he thought. Her own personal Garden of Eden. And suddenly he pictured her walking naked through the garden, her red hair cascading over her pale breasts, pausing to pluck an apple from a tree. He braced his arm against one of those trees and tried to stop his wildly beating heart. Heat spread through his limbs like wildfire.

He should never have come here. And he should have kept his hands off of her. This whole thing was a terrible mistake. Back home he would never have had these erotic thoughts about Carrie. She was his partner, and she would be again, if he had anything to say about it. Though as each day passed, he felt he had less and less to say about it. He felt he was falling deeper and deeper into a hole. First it was an engagement, then a wedding, and now...a baby. Maybe he should forget about Carrie, wish her well and go home. Home, without her? Work, without her? He had to admit it, the future looked bleak without her, without her comments, her insight, her optimism. Her smile that turned him inside out. He set the lunch bag on the table and went to the hammock and gave it a gentle push. Her smile deepened and she sighed contentedly. "Carrie, lunch. Wake up."

She opened her eyes. "What's wrong with me?" she asked, blinking at the sunshine dappled across the patio. "I don't take naps."

"What about the time we were on a stakeout for three days in Beverly Hills in front of that jewelry store? You took a nap every afternoon."

"Because I was awake all night while you slept," she reminded him.

She got out of the hammock and sat down in one of the patio chairs. Then she dug into the brown paper bag. "Mmm, tuna salad on cracked wheat, my favorite." She bit into her sandwich and looked at him. "You know a lot about me, don't you?"

"Considering we've been partners for so long, I guess I do."

"But I don't know anything about you. Until today."

"It doesn't matter."

"It does to me. I understand you better."

He frowned. "I don't want to be understood."

"Then you shouldn't have come here. Because you haven't got your uniform to hide behind or your apartment to go home to at night. You may be at great risk of being understood here, God forbid."

"You're right," he admitted, "but it's worth it if I can stop you from making a big mistake."

"That's what you think, isn't it? That I'm making a mistake just because it's something you'd never do."

"You said I know a lot about you. Well, I do. I know what you like on your sandwiches, and I know you sleep with your hand under your cheek, and I also know that you thrive on danger and excitement. That you're smart and savvy and you'd be wasted on a town like this." He leaned forward in his chair and pounded his fist on the table. He didn't mean to get so worked up, but he didn't know how else to get through to her.

"*Thrived* on danger, but not anymore. Now I thrive on crime prevention and walking to work and swinging in a hammock on my lunch hour. I told you I'd do anything to get this job and I meant it. I'll cut ribbons at the opening of grocery stores, and I'll get married in a dress that's been hanging in a museum for a hundred years. I'll do anything to get out . . . to get away from . . . from . . ."

"From what—crime, violence . . . me?"

"Yes. I mean, no. Why would I want to get away from you?" She hoped he didn't suspect, hoped she could get through the remaining days without him guessing how she felt about him. Because it was getting harder and harder to pretend. And to hide her feelings. Somehow when she pictured this tryout, this audition, she hadn't realized how much time they would be spending together. Day *and* night.

"I'm not the easiest person to get along with," he said, crushing his empty soda can in his hand. "But if you come back, I'll change." His gaze, level and serious, caught hers. "I won't nag you about missing target practice or not filling out your time sheet right."

"It's not about that, Matt." She braced her elbows on the small table. "You can't change. Any more than I can. And I don't want you to. But I can't live there anymore, or work with you anymore. It's nothing personal." Nothing personal. Oh, no. Nothing except the way she watched him when he wasn't looking, worried about him when he went home alone at night, thought about him on weekends, dreamt about him at night.

His expression was unreadable, his eyes the color of smoke. Then he straightened in his chair. "I may have to leave early," he said abruptly.

She looked at her watch. "I'll go with you. I have to be back at one o'clock."

"I mean, I might not be able to stick it out for two weeks."

She got to her feet and crumpled the brown paper lunch bag. "Is it that bad?" she asked. Maybe he found all this togetherness just as uncomfortable as she did. He must.

"It's not bad," he said, standing next to her. "It's just not me."

Carrie wavered. She wanted to tell him to go. That she didn't want him, didn't need him anymore. If he weren't there, she could start the job of forgetting him, start getting used to life without him. As long as he was around, she clung to some small shred of hope that one day he would notice her. Not as a partner, but as a woman. And he had. Unless that scene in the car was really to impress some invisible person. And now that he'd noticed her, she wanted more. She wanted him to love her. Oh, not the way she loved him, just some fraction of that. But that was wishful thinking. That would never happen.

"I understand," she said. And she did. What a pain to have to put up with her enthusing over every blade of grass, every wisp of fog, every breath of fresh air here, which had to call into question the life-style he'd chosen for himself. "I just hope you can make it to the dress rehearsal."

He didn't answer. They walked back to city hall, and he paused at the front steps.

"I'll pick you up tonight. Five o'clock?"

They both knew that they never left work on time back home. That was just another obvious advantage to coming here. If you liked predictability, dull routine. Personally, Matt preferred the unknown, the unexpected.

He got into his car and headed back to the B and B, restless, bored, annoyed with himself and with Carrie and with the whole town for taking her away from him.

As he pulled up in front of the brown-shingled inn with the riot of marigolds tumbling over the front fence, he noticed a ladder propped against the side of the house. Mandy Clayton was on top of the ladder, a paintbrush in one hand and a bucket of paint in the other. Her tunic top was stretched over her expanding stomach.

As Matt watched, Adam came around the corner of the house and caught a glimpse of her. He stopped in his tracks and yelled at her to come down. She yelled back that she would come down when she was finished. Matt got out of the car and leaned against the side door, watching while they discussed the advisability of her coming down immediately versus her continuing until the job was done. When she finally descended, slowly, laboriously, in her own good time, with Adam gripping the sides of the ladder tightly, she pretended to dump the bucket of paint on his head. He took the bucket of paint, lifted her in his arms and carried her into the house.

They didn't see Matt. They were in their own world, just the two of them. Two and a half, actually. Matt felt an uncomfortable, unfamiliar feeling lurking between his shoulder blades as he walked up the driveway. What it was, he didn't know. It couldn't be envy. A pregnant wife was the last thing in the world he wanted. And he didn't want that kind of intimacy, that warmth or understanding, either. Of course not. Those were luxuries he couldn't afford. It was

fine if you led a carefree, relaxed life as proprietors of a
B and B on the edge of the sea, with nobody depending on
you to save their life, to recover their stolen belongings or
rescue them from a crazed gunman.

Matt walked around the side of the house to the terrace
facing the sea and sat in a deck chair the hosts had
thoughtfully placed to take advantage of the view of sky
and sea. He was thinking about Carrie and how she had
managed to get him talking about his childhood. He'd
thought dredging up memories would throw him into depression, but after telling her, he felt only relief. As if he'd
meant to tell her sometime, and he'd finally gotten around
to it. But he hadn't meant to tell anybody. Ever.

He was still puzzling over it when Adam came out the
back door carrying two cold beers. "You look like you
could use one of these," Adam said, setting the can on the
table between them. "Hard day?"

"I'm not used to vacations," Matt said, shifting rest-
lessly in his chair.

Adam nodded understandingly, sprawled in a lounge
chair and took a long sip of his beer. "That's how I felt
when I first came here. I was a workaholic. Yeah, I'd been
in the Yukon drilling for oil for eight months straight.
Suddenly I was on R and R at Mandy's B and B."

Matt looked at him in surprise. "And you never left?"

"I left for a rig in the North Sea. But not for long. It
didn't take long to realize the thrills of hundred-mile-per-
hour winds and minus zero temperatures were vastly overrated."

"And now you're..." Matt trailed off.

"Go ahead and say it. Mandy's hired hand." He
laughed. "Cook, dishwasher and soon...tah-dah...baby-
sitter."

Matt stared at him in disbelief. A wildcatting oil driller,
a geologist, reduced to working at his wife's bed and

breakfast? Either the guy had a very strong ego or none at all. The former seemed more likely.

"Anyway, I recommend marrying a woman with a job. They're happier and more secure. But you've already figured that out. What did you say you were planning to do here?"

Matt hunched his shoulders up around his collar like a turtle trying to hide. "I don't know. I haven't decided yet. I might...open a coffeehouse," he said idly.

"On Main Street, with live music on weekends?" Adam asked.

"Sure, why not?"

"That would be a real addition to the town," Adam enthused. "You know you can't get a decent cup of coffee around here unless you make it yourself."

Matt smiled wryly. "I thought so."

There was a long companionable silence while they drank beer and looked out at the fishing boats bobbing in the blue Pacific water.

"Ever try it?" Adam asked, setting his empty can on the ground.

"What, fishing?"

He shook his head. "Parenthood."

Matt almost choked on his last swig. "No, I can't say I have. Do you recommend it?"

"Oh, God, I don't know. I'm scared out of my mind. Scared for Mandy, scared for myself." He wiped his brow with his sleeve. "I never saw myself as the domestic type. But here I am with a house and a wife, and pretty soon, this baby."

Matt studied his face, remembered the laughter, the concern he'd heard in Adam's voice as he'd called to his wife. "Doesn't look like you're too unhappy about it," he noted.

"I've never been happier in my life. I thought I had it all. Freedom, adventure. But that was nothing, nothing com-

pared to what I have here with Mandy…and now this kid."
A slow smile creased his face.

"The icing on the cake," Matt muttered. Well, it might
work for Adam, but some people just weren't cut out for
it.

"You planning on starting a family?" Adam asked.

Matt cleared his throat. "I don't think so. Carrie takes
her career very seriously."

"So does Mandy. She thought she wouldn't have time for
a baby. I had to talk her into it."

Matt raised his eyebrows. "*You* talked her into it?"

"Yep. Told her we'd do it together. I knew how much she
wanted one. Just mention the word baby and she'd get this
look in her eyes."

The look. The faraway look Matt had seen in Carrie's
eyes just that morning when they'd discussed the nursery.
He clenched his hands into fists and got to his feet. This
conversation was getting positively weird. "Thanks for the
beer," he said.

"Sure. Hey, if you get a chance, take a look at the
building on the corner of Third and Main. There's an old
saloon there from before the town went dry that'd make a
great coffeehouse. See what you think."

Matt hesitated. "I'm not sure I'm cut out to run a business. I've been a public servant all these years."

Adam studied him from the depths of his lounge chair.
"Maybe it's time for a change."

"You sound like Carrie," he remarked.

"By the way," Adam said, getting to his feet. "When do
you need your laundry?"

Laundry. The granny gown. So that's where it went. "No
rush. In fact we don't need it until we leave. Keep it at the
bottom of your pile."

Adam nodded and Matt went around the house and got
in his car. He didn't know where he was going. He just
knew he couldn't sit there any longer and pretend to be

someone he wasn't. The trouble was, he was having a hard time remembering who he was.

Carrie looked up from her desk and out the window. It was almost five o'clock and she'd just finished polishing her speech for the Elks club that night. She wished Matt wasn't coming to get her. The less time she spent with him, the better. She didn't want any more memories getting in the way of her new life.

Would she ever forget waking up beside him at the inn? Yes, she had to. She had to forget how he looked with his hair on end, his face creased with lines from the pillow, his eyes at half-mast. He'd changed. She'd changed. He wasn't her hero anymore. He was less and yet he was more. Behind that uniform there was a real, vulnerable man. A man who needed someone to love him. He would never admit it, but she'd seen the longing in his eyes, the sorrow when he talked about his childhood.

The mayor knocked on her door and interrupted her reverie by asking Carrie how everything was going.

"Fine, but is there any reason…do you have any doubts about my ability to do the job?" she asked. She had to know.

"In other words," the gray-haired woman said, taking a seat across from Carrie's desk, "when are we going to finalize our offer to you? I want you to know you're everything we hoped you'd be. Young, enthusiastic and tough on crime. There's just one thing… Does your fiancé really like it here?"

"Oh, yes," Carrie said quickly, maybe too quickly. "It's just taking him a while to find himself."

"To find himself a job," the mayor added. "I've been thinking, he's too young to retire."

"Right," Carrie agreed. What irony, she thought. She couldn't get the job without Matt, and now Matt was standing in her way. They had to see she was the perfect candidate for the job. She had everything they wanted. No husband, no fiancé and no baby to stand in her way of performing her professional duties. Her job was her life. Her commitment to the community would be absolute. And yet they wanted her to have a husband for stability. And now her husband had to have a job. What next?

No more was said about Matt's job before the mayor left work that night, but the question weighed heavily on Carrie. When she walked out the front door to meet Matt, she said, "I don't really want to go back to the inn." She didn't want to go anywhere or do anything. Young, enthusiastic? She felt old and tired. Tired of playing this game.

"Where, then?" he asked. "We've been to the beach. What else is there? If we were in L.A., we could take in a gallery, an early show or a museum."

"As if we ever did those things," Carrie said. "I was always too busy. Working and then school. But it paid off. Look where it got me."

"Yeah," he said, looking up and down the quiet street. "Well, now that you're here, what are you going to do?"

"The problem is, what are *you* going to do? That's what the mayor wants to know. Let's go get the local newspaper and see what's in the want ads."

"Is that really necessary?"

"You don't have to *take* a job, you just have to *find* one," she explained.

He grimaced, but he walked up the street with her toward the newsstand.

When they'd bought the modest weekly newspaper, Matt suggested walking down to the harbor to a wooden bench where they could watch the fishermen unload their boats. The smell of tar and salt water and fresh fish was in the air.

"Don't you love it?" Carrie asked, feeling her enthusiasm creep back. "I mean, it's not a yacht harbor for the idle rich. It's a real, working operation."

He didn't disagree. He just watched the men grapple with huge nets full of silverback salmon. Carrie opened the paper and turned to the three meager Help Wanted columns.

"Not quite the L.A. *Times*," he noted, looking over her shoulder.

"Nothing's as big as it is in L.A.," she said huffily. "You don't have to keep reminding me. The newspaper's small, the town is small. That's why I'm here. Because it's small and safe and it's real."

"You don't quit, do you?" he asked with an amused look in his gray eyes. "I know you like it here."

"And I know you don't," she countered. "Here's something. Nursery school teacher. The hours are good. Nine to three."

"Is this the kind of nursery for kids or plants?" he asked, stretching his legs out in front of him.

"Which would you prefer?" she asked, spreading the paper out in front of her.

"I don't get along with either very well."

She lowered the paper to look at him. She wanted to say he would be better off working at either one than in the streets of L.A. and he'd live longer. But she knew better than to harp on the same old theme. Anyway it wasn't for real, this job search, but she wished it was. She wished so hard she didn't realize she'd squeezed her eyes shut tight.

"Give me that paper," he said, breaking into her trance. "How can you read it with your eyes closed?"

She handed it to him, and when his fingers brushed hers, she felt a current of energy leap from him to her and back again. He felt it, too. She saw it in the flicker of awareness in his eyes, heard it in the tone of his voice when he finally spoke.

He cleared his throat. "Short Order Cook. Mulligan's Pancake House. Weekends. That's no good." He leaned toward her to show her the ad and his shoulder pressed against hers.

She felt the warmth of his body and she longed to put her head on his shoulder, feel his arm around her and ease away the tension of the day.

"Cold?" he asked as the wind stirred the water on the bay and blew a wisp of hair across her cheek. Without waiting for an answer he took off his sweater and handed it to her.

She stood and put it on, grateful for the warmth of his body still clinging to the wool. His eyes lingered on the extra-large sweater that swallowed her up and his gaze warmed her even more than the sweater. She sat down abruptly and stared at the newspaper. "What's wrong with pancakes?" she asked, bringing herself back to the problem at hand.

"I can't work weekends," he explained. "I'd never get to see the kid."

She blinked. "Oh, the hypothetical baby." He wasn't going to let her forget. "You ought to have a people job, you know," she said, anxious to change the subject.

"Why? The only people I'm good at working with is you."

She turned her head toward him to protest. He was looking at her with a devastating half smile. His eyes reflected the deep blue water in the late afternoon sun. He slanted his head so his lips were inches from hers. The paper slipped out of her hands and onto the ground. She thought he was going to kiss her, right here in front of the sea gulls.

But the fishermen had left. There was no one to impress. So why was he doing this? And why did she want him to? She knew how it would feel. She remembered the warmth, the urgency, of his kisses. She would never forget them. But there couldn't be any more. It would only make things more difficult when he left.

She reached for the newspaper and folded it carefully. "You're right," she said, staring at the columns of ads for

❖ SILHOUETTE™

AN IMPORTANT MESSAGE FROM THE EDITORS OF SILHOUETTE®

Dear Reader,

Because you've chosen to read one of our fine romance novels, we'd like to say "thank you"! And, as a **special** way to thank you, we've selected <u>four more</u> of the <u>books</u> you love so well, **and** a Porcelain Trinket Box to send you absolutely ***FREE!***

Please enjoy them with our compliments...

Anne Canadeo
Senior Editor,
Silhouette Romance

P.S. And <u>because</u> we value our customers, we've attached something extra inside ...

EDITOR'S
FREE
GIFT
SEAL
THANK YOU

PEEL OFF SEAL AND PLACE INSIDE

HOW TO VALIDATE YOUR
EDITOR'S FREE GIFT "THANK YOU"

1. Peel off gift seal from front cover. Place it in space provided at right. This automatically entitles you to receive four free books and a beautiful Porcelain Trinket Box.

2. Send back this card and you'll get brand-new Silhouette Romance™ novels. These books have a cover price of $2.99 each, but they are yours to keep absolutely free.

3. There's no catch. You're under no obligation to buy anything. We charge nothing—ZERO—for your first shipment. And you don't have to make any minimum number of purchases—not even one!

4. The fact is thousands of readers enjoy receiving books by mail from the Silhouette Reader Service™ months before they're available in stores. They like the convenience of home delivery and they love our discount prices!

5. We hope that after receiving your free books you'll want to remain a subscriber. But the choice is yours—to continue or cancel, anytime at all! So why not take us up on our invitation, with no risk of any kind. You'll be glad you did!

6. Don't forget to detach your FREE BOOKMARK. And remember...just for validating your Editor's Free Gift Offer, we'll send you FIVE MORE gifts, *ABSOLUTELY FREE!*

YOURS FREE!

*This beautiful porcelain box is topped with a lovely bouquet of porcelain flowers, perfect for holding rings, pins or other precious trinkets — and is yours **absolutely free** when you accept our no risk offer!*

THE EDITOR'S "THANK YOU" FREE GIFTS INCLUDE:

▶ Four BRAND-NEW romance novels
▶ A Porcelain Trinket Box

THE SILHOUETTE READER SERVICE™: HERE'S HOW IT WORKS

Accepting free books places you under no obligation to buy anything. You may keep the books and gift and return the shipping statement marked "cancel". If you do not cancel, about a month later we will send you 6 additional novels, and bill you just $2.44 each plus 25¢ delivery and applicable sales tax, if any.* That's the complete price, and—compared to cover prices of $2.99 each—quite a bargain! You may cancel at any time, but if you choose to continue, every month we'll send you 6 more books, which you may either purchase at the discount price...or return at our expense and cancel your subscription.

*Terms and prices subject to change without notice. Sales tax applicable in N.Y.

If offer card is missing write to: Silhouette Reader Service, 3010 Walden Ave., P.O. Box 1867, Buffalo, NY 14269-1867

BUSINESS REPLY MAIL
FIRST CLASS MAIL   PERMIT NO. 717   BUFFALO, NY

POSTAGE WILL BE PAID BY ADDRESSEE

SILHOUETTE READER SERVICE
3010 WALDEN AVE
PO BOX 1867
BUFFALO NY 14240-9952

NO POSTAGE
NECESSARY
IF MAILED
IN THE
UNITED STATES

stuffing envelopes at home and part-time gardeners. "There's nothing for you here." She stood. "Anyway, I have to be at the Elks club in a half hour. You're invited, of course. It's a free dinner."

"There's no such thing as a free dinner," he told her. "Don't you know that? The price is that we've got to eat rubber chicken followed by the swill they call coffee around here."

They walked slowly back down the pier and into town. "If I ever hear you say something good about this place, I think I'll faint," Carrie said.

"Don't do that," he warned. "Police chiefs might pass out, but they never faint. Not unless they have someone to catch them." He tousled her hair playfully and a ridiculous giddy feeling left her feeling light-headed. Why? Because Matt Graham, her tough, no-nonsense partner, teased her. But it wasn't just that. It was a sudden euphoria, a feeling that there was something there between them, something rare and wonderful.

And then, just as quickly as it came, it was gone. Replaced by the knowledge that this two-week vacation would soon be over, and while she'd come out of it with a new job and a new life, she would lose Matt in the bargain. She knew it. She'd always known it. But she couldn't help the sadness creeping into her heart.

She almost wished Matt would leave early. Because she couldn't take much more of this. Of these glimpses into his past and into his soul. Of these nights in the same bed or intimate dinners for two. It was better to eat potluck with the whole town or the Elks. But could she find a new group to eat with every night? Could she endure another night in that honeymoon suite? She just hoped her granny gown would be back from wherever it went.

Chapter Six

Matt went with Carrie to the Elks club dinner. The food was terrible and the coffee worse. He didn't know why he was at the dinner. He didn't know why he was in Moss Beach. It wasn't his kind of place. It was too small, too personal and too hokey. He had to admit Carrie's speech was good, though. She charmed everyone in the place including him with her candor and her modesty. She came across as tough and tender at the same time. Which was exactly what she was, he realized, watching her take questions.

"You must be a mighty brave woman to be in police work," one older resident said. "Are you afraid of anything?"

Carrie's eyes sought Matt's at the table at the back of the room, as if she were afraid he would jump up and say she was afraid of spiders, or maybe she was just seeking his advice. But she didn't need his advice on how to field questions from a crowd. She was doing fine.

"Of course I'm afraid every time I put on my uniform and go out on the street. But it's not the kind of fear that paralyzes, it's the kind that just makes you watch your step. That keeps you alert. It's a constructive fear." After she answered some more questions, the president gave her a bouquet of flowers and the club's endorsement as their next police chief.

Matt was filled with sudden pride. As if it was really his fiancée up there shaking hands and accepting good wishes. But it was just his partner. Former partner. When she'd finally shaken every hand in the house, he put her bouquet in the trunk along with his sweater and they drove back to the inn in silence. Matt was still wondering what it would take to change Carrie's mind.

He had no idea how to break up this love affair between Carrie and the town. Of course it wouldn't last. In a few months she would realize what a mistake she'd made and come running back to him. The idea brought a smile to his lips. But by then he would have a new partner. His smile faded. He had to think of some way to convince her now. However, he had a hard time thinking clearly when he was around her. All he could do was to make jokes about the town and watch her protest. Watch her cheeks redden and her eyes flash. Yes, he enjoyed teasing her. He enjoyed sleeping in the same bed with her, eating with her, and that wasn't all he enjoyed.

When they arrived at the inn, the front door swung open and Adam called to him. "Matt, is that you? Telephone."

"What?" he asked, turning off the ignition. "Nobody knows I'm here."

Carrie watched him walk to the front door. She let herself out and opened the trunk to pick up her flowers. Her hand brushed against leather, shoe leather. She dropped the flowers and peered into the trunk. Her shoes. Those were her shoes half-hidden under a golf towel. So Matt had played a trick on her by hiding her shoes. Just to see what she would do. Just to see how she would solve the crime.

It couldn't be that he was trying to make her look bad in front of the town. Take away her footwear on the night of the big potluck dinner. It couldn't be that he was desperate for her to return with him to L.A. She wanted to believe he would do anything to keep her with him. That he didn't want to lose her. That he couldn't live without her. She stood there, running her fingers over the soft leather until she came to her senses. It was a prank, a practical joke, that was all.

She would have liked to march into the inn with the shoes in her hand and demand an answer. But then she would find out the truth. He would tell her he'd found the shoes abandoned in a trash can. This way maybe she could cling to her fantasies a little longer. That was all she had left.

Mandy, looking radiant in an ankle-length maternity hostess gown, greeted Carrie at the door. "What lovely flowers. Let me get you a vase. Matt's on the phone in the kitchen," she said, reaching into the cabinet for a vase and filling it with water from the wet bar. "Sounds important," she whispered conspiratorily to Carrie. "It gives me the chills to think of him giving up his job to follow you up here."

"It does?" Carrie asked, giving the flowers to Mandy and sinking into the deep cushions of the couch.

"We get a lot of couples here," Mandy confided, arranging the roses artfully, "but none more in love than you two."

It must be hormones, Carrie thought, that make her think that. Only a woman in the last stages of pregnancy would be fooled into thinking Matt was in love with her.

"Mandy." Adam leaned over the banister from the second floor and motioned to her. "It's past your bedtime," he said sternly.

Mandy wrinkled her nose and rolled her eyes heavenward. "Honestly, you'd think no one had ever been pregnant before," she said to Carrie. "I'm coming," she called. "There's coffee on the stove and sherry in the liquor cabinet. Help yourselves." Then she dimmed the lights, raked the coals in the fireplace, and went up the stairs.

Carrie accepted the invitation and went to pour herself a glass of sherry. Then she kicked off her athletic shoes and tucked her legs underneath her on the couch. When Matt came into the room a few minutes later his face was grim.

"What is it? Who was it?" she asked, setting her glass on the coffee table.

"That was Buck Quin back at the station. My apartment was broken into."

"Did they take anything?" she asked, a cold chill running up her spine.

He sat down next to her and ran his hands through his hair. "There wasn't much to take. They left something, though. A message."

"What do you mean?" she demanded. "Is it someone you know?"

"Someone who knows me. Someone I testified against a few years ago. Just got out on parole."

"Oh, God." Carrie buried her head in her hands.

"Don't worry," he said, gently lifting her hands from her face. "I wasn't there. If I'd been there I would have got him before he got me."

"How do you know?" The thought of Matt being shot while he slept in his tiny, impersonal apartment with no one to hear him cry out, no one to care, was more than she could bear. She started to cry, helplessly, feeling stupid and childish.

"Carrie," said Matt calmly. "I'm okay. Nothing happened." Through her tears she saw confusion and surprise on his face. She pressed her lips together, but she couldn't stop the tears from streaming down her cheeks.

"I know n-nothing happened," she stammered, fumbling for a tissue. "But when you go back he'll be waiting for you." She gripped his shoulder. "You can't go back. He'll get you."

"I'll move. I was going to move anyway. This isn't like you," he said, reaching for his handkerchief and handing it to her. "You've seen blood and guts and gore. You never fall apart. What's wrong?"

Her hand fell away from his shoulder and he wiped a tear from her cheek. Her lower lip trembled. "If anything happened to you," she said and then stopped. If anything happened to him, she didn't know what she would do. He was her strength and her idol.

"If anything happened to me, you'd have to find another fiancé, is that what's worrying you?"

She drew a shaky breath. "That's right. I had a hard enough time finding you."

"Look," he said patiently. "I'm here and this guy is there. They've probably picked him up by now for parole violation." He lifted her glass from the table. "Here, drink your sherry and we'll go to bed."

She reached for the glass and as her hand met his they both realized what he'd said. She knew he didn't mean it the way it sounded and yet . . . the look in his eyes told her he did. A spark leapt from a drying log in the fireplace and sizzled in the dry air.

She should say something, something light and humorous to break the tension, but she couldn't. She wanted to go to bed with him. Wanted to have him carry her up the stairs, undress her with his warm, strong hands and make passionate love to her until the sun rose over the hills and shone on their naked bodies. She felt the heat rise up and color her cheeks. But she couldn't tear her eyes from his.

The all-knowing look in his smoky gray eyes told her he knew exactly what she was thinking. But how could he? Unless he was thinking the same thing. Which he couldn't

be. He was just trying to calm her. But it wasn't working.
She was strung as tight as a guitar string just waiting to be
plucked. How much longer could she endure this torture,
this game of pretend, before she slipped up and let him see
how she felt about him, how she'd always felt about him?

She picked up her glass and brought it to her lips. She
forced herself to sip her sherry calmly, deliberately, then set
her glass down. He was watching her with narrowed eyes as
if he were trying to figure her out. There was nothing to
figure out. She was there to get a job, he was there to help
her out. Or was he? What about her shoes? What about
getting her lost on the way to work so she was late? If she
didn't know better she would think he was trying to come
between her and her new job. But she'd already dismissed
that possibility. Her mind was like a hamster on an exer-
cise wheel, going around and around and never getting
anywhere.

"Ready?" he asked, standing and holding out his hand
to her.

Ready? She would never be ready. Not for another night
in that bedroom, in that bed with him. The first night she
should have turned around and walked out, slept in the car
or on the beach, anywhere but next to him. Ready? The
word echoed off the walls of the living room. She couldn't
ignore it any longer...or his outstretched hand. Like a
sleepwalker, she held out her hand; he pulled her up, and
they walked up the stairs.

Once inside the room she realized to her dismay that her
old nightgown still wasn't back from the laundry or wherever it had gone. Matt stood leaning against the door, one
hand on the doorknob.

"I'm going back down to make a call."

"You're calling the station, aren't you? You *are* worried."

"I'm not worried. I have to talk to Buck, that's all." He
closed the door quietly behind him.

On the phone in Mandy's kitchen, Matt asked Buck if he thought the guy was armed.

"What do you think?" Buck asked. "He's not going after you with a bow and arrow. He's out for revenge."

"Maybe I ought to come back."

"That's just what you shouldn't do. You're safer up there, and you're not on this case, I am. Besides, you've got no place to come back to. This guy is serious. He messed up your place pretty good. Shot holes through your mattress where you would have been sleeping."

"Uh-huh."

"So don't let it spoil your vacation."

"A crazed gunman is out to get me, but no, I won't let it spoil my vacation, of course not."

"What's it like up there?"

"Quiet, very quiet."

"What do you do for fun?"

Follow Carrie around. Fantasize about making love to her. "Well, there's the beach. We watch the tide come in...and go out."

"Pretty exciting stuff." Buck guffawed. "Is that all? I heard you went up there with your partner, Carrie. I didn't know you two were..."

"We're not. Where'd you hear that?"

"At the soda machine. She there with you?"

"She's here, but not with me." Well, technically she wasn't with him. She was upstairs. He was down.

Upstairs in bed in a pale green silk nightgown, waiting for him. Yeah, sure. Good God, was the whole station talking about them, speculating about why they'd gone off together? He should have thought of that sooner, planted some story before he'd left. But since he didn't think of her as anything but a partner, why would anyone else? "She's...around somewhere," he said vaguely. "Hey, keep me posted, will you?"

Buck said he would and Matt hung up. He walked up the stairs slowly. He didn't like the sound of this guy out on parole. He was more worried about him than he let Carrie or Buck know. He remembered now that he'd threatened to get even the day he got out. That day had come. Never mind. He was there; Matt was here, thanks to Carrie. He opened the bedroom door softly. Carrie was in bed, propped up against a pillow, reading a book.

"What did they say?"

"Nothing. They'll keep me posted. There's nothing to worry about."

"Right. Some psycho is out to kill you, but there's nothing to worry about. Admit it, you're glad you came with me, because if not . . ." She shivered.

He sat on the edge of the bed and took his shoes off. "If I'd been there I would have taken care of him."

"Sure you would. Do you sleep with a gun under your pillow?"

"No, not usually. I really don't want to talk about it," he said, walking into the bathroom with his overnight bag. He'd been brusque with her. He could tell she'd felt snubbed, but he didn't want to think about what would have happened if he'd been there. He *wasn't* there.

He came back out of the bathroom in his boxers. Carrie didn't look up from her book. There was a definite frost in the air. He pulled the blanket back and crawled into bed. He crossed his arms under his head and stared straight ahead. The silence lay heavy and uncomfortable between them. He turned his head in her direction.

"What are you reading?" he asked.

She didn't look at him. *"Gulliver's Travels."*

"Is it good?"

"I don't know. I just started it. I found it in the book-case over there," she said coolly, pointing toward the shelves.

He slid a glance in her direction. Despite the sheet and blanket pulled up around her shoulders, he knew she was wearing the nightgown he'd given her. But what good did it do if he couldn't see her in it? He could imagine how she would look, however. And that was as close as he was going to get. Right now Gulliver's journey seemed like nothing compared to the trip across this enormous bed to where she was. She turned a page nonchalantly, as if he wasn't there.

She might be worried about his safety, but that didn't mean she was interested in him personally. Or did it? There were times when her brown eyes warmed at something he said or something he did, and a flush crept up her freckled face. But it was obvious her new job came first with her and that she had no need for a real husband or a partner.

So that left him with nothing. No partner and not even his bare-bones apartment. Self-pity was something he'd never indulged in and he wasn't going to start now. Not envy, either. Not envy for Carrie's new job, house and town. Who would want to be stuck in Moss Beach for the rest of his life anyway? Not him.

The room was quiet except for the sound of the sea pounding on the rocks below the cliff and the rustle of the pages turning, turning so fast she must be either a speed reader or she'd lost her place. He propped his head on his hand and looked at Carrie, unable to pretend, as she did, that he didn't exist. "What's it about?" he asked.

"A man who takes a trip," she said.

"Like me," he observed.

"He goes by ship instead of car," she explained, her eyes on her book.

"Go on," he urged.

"Here," she said, handing the book to him. "You read it. I'm going to sleep." She snapped off her bedside lamp, leaving only a night-light by the door.

There was a knock on the door. Carrie slid down under the covers.

"Carrie?" said Adam. "Can I come in? I've got a message for you."

Matt tossed the book on the floor and took Carrie by the arm to pull her across the wide expanse of smooth, percale sheet toward him. She stiffened, protesting under her breath.

"What are you doing?" she whispered.

"You don't want him to get the wrong idea, do you?" he asked under his breath. He wrapped his arms around her until her back was pressed against his chest, her curved bottom cradled in his hips.

"No, but really…"

"Come on in, Adam," Matt said, his fingers tracing the underside of her full breasts through the silkiness of the nightgown. This might be his only opportunity to enjoy the new nightgown.

She gasped and drew her knees up against her chest. Adam opened the door and stood in the doorway. "Sorry to disturb you folks," he said, squinting into the darkened room. "But the mayor called and said there's a problem down at the campground. She knows it's not your job, Carrie, not yet. But she asked if you could just have a look. Some drunk disturbing the campers."

"Oh, uh, sure, of course." She couldn't move, not with Matt's arm firmly around her waist, his warm breath against her ear and his hands making her feel like a jelly-fish floating in the tide. She couldn't move, and she didn't want to move. She wanted to stay right there, in his arms. She wanted to feel his hands cupping her aching breasts, then tease the sensitive tips…but she *had* to move. Duty called. If she could show the town she could handle an emergency, maybe they'd forget about her fiancé and his lack of employment.

"Thanks, Adam," she said, proud of how steady her voice was. "I'll go right away." As soon as she extricated herself from Matt's arms. As soon as she transformed back into an officer of the law instead of a sex-starved female. But Matt was ahead of her. He was out of bed and dressed in the dark before she was.

"What are you doing?" she asked as she stuffed her legs into a pair of long pants, taking advantage of the darkness to take off her nightgown and put on a sweatshirt.

"Going with you," he said. "What did you think? That I'd let you face some crazed drunk by yourself? You didn't even bring your gun, did you?"

"I didn't think..." She sat down on the bed to put her shoes on. "This is my job," she insisted.

"I know, but I'm still your partner. Until you officially resign."

She stood and opened the door. "All right, but don't you dare get in my way."

Carrie knew where the park was so she directed while Matt drove down a dirt road to a scenic spot along the beach. The lights of a dozen campers glowed in the dark as they pulled in at the entrance. Through the still night air they could hear a scratchy voice yelling obscenities. In the beam of Carrie's flashlight there was a tall, scrawny figure of a man waving a bottle in one hand.

Carrie's heart was pumping madly. This disturbance was nothing compared to the L.A. variety, but it was her first chance to show what she could do in a real crime situation. She walked up to the man, feeling Matt's presence behind her, knowing he was probably armed, and wishing he wasn't there at all. She didn't need a backup.

"Sir," she said in her most official tone. "This is a private campground and the consumption of alcohol is forbidden by city ordinance."

He waved his bottle at her menacingly and before she could say another word, Matt was behind him, backhanding him until he'd dropped the bottle harmlessly in the dirt.

"Hey," he protested. "That's mine."

"Not anymore," Matt said.

The other campers gathered around and cheered loudly, while Carrie watched helplessly. They'd cheered for Matt. It was her job, but he'd done it. She should have left him behind in bed. Better yet, she should have left him in L.A. Carrie called the sheriff from the public phone at the campground, and he promised to come and take the man to the county jail. Carrie then called the mayor and told her the matter was taken care of. She didn't elaborate, but she was sure the mayor would find out who'd *really* taken care of the matter.

An hour later Matt and Carrie were on their way back to the inn.

"I guess you think I butted in," Matt said after a long silence. "But I thought he was going to hit you over the head."

"I wouldn't have let him," she said, anger rising in her throat. "Believe me, I can take care of myself. I shouldn't have to spell it out for you of all people."

"I'm sorry. I don't know what got into me. When he raised his arm, I lost it. All I could think was that you weren't armed."

"Neither was he."

"You didn't know that," he protested.

"For the last time, Matt, this isn't L.A. Maybe you ought to go back there." It may have sounded ungrateful, but she'd had it with his overprotectiveness.

"Maybe I should," he retorted.

"Fine with me," she answered, clenching her hands against the seat. He never used to treat her like a fragile flower. Somewhere along the line he'd lost his respect for her as an officer. He'd gone all macho on her, protecting her from a harmless drunk as if she'd never been to the police academy, never taken martial arts, never confronted an actual inebriate before.

The sooner he left, the better off she would be. The longer he stayed, the harder it was for her to deny the attraction she felt for him. The harder it was going to be to keep it hidden from him. On the other hand, she didn't want him to leave until she had the job sewn up. Which showed how hard-hearted and selfish she was. She knew it, and he knew it, too. She clasped her hands together in her lap and they rode home in silence.

Carrie fell asleep as soon as her head hit the pillow, worn out from the physical and emotional upheavals of the day. She'd thought life would be simple here along the coast, but instead it was unbelievably complicated. Which wasn't Moss Beach's fault. It was Matt Graham's fault, whose very life would be in danger if he went back to L.A. How could she even suggest such a thing! In the morning she would tell him she was sorry for what she'd said.

In the middle of the night Matt rolled over and let out a terrified shout. She sat up straight and stared at him, allowing one strap of green silk to slip off her shoulder. With a strangled voice he called her and kicked off the blankets with violent, jerky movements. She reached for him, but he pushed her away with his wildly thrashing arms.

She scrambled across the bed and grabbed him by the shoulders. "Matt, it's me, Carrie. What's wrong?" she demanded, her hair tumbling over her forehead.

He opened his eyes without seeing her. "He got me," he said. "I couldn't . . ." He shuddered and she pulled him to her, holding him against her, his chest against her breasts.

He drew a ragged breath. "Oh, God, Carrie. It scared the hell out of me."

"It was a nightmare," she said, pulling back to look at his face. "You're okay." His eyes came into focus, and he wrapped his arms around her. The hair on his chest rubbed against her bare breast and she felt faint. If he weren't holding her, she might just pass out. Her heart lurched. His heart beat against hers like a jungle drum.

He pulled her down on top of him and rolled onto his side, holding her to him as if he'd never let her go. "This is real?" he asked hoarsely. "I didn't die and go to heaven?"

She took his face in her hands. "This is real," she said, looking deep into his eyes. But in fact she wasn't so sure. *She* might be the one who was dreaming, lying there half-naked in her partner's arms.

Awkwardly she hiked her strap back onto her shoulder and inched her way over to her side of the bed. He was fine now. She could tell by the way he was looking at her, with relief taking the place of anxiety. He almost looked embarrassed that she'd seen him in a moment of weakness. She attempted to give him a reassuring smile, one that would convince him she still respected him, still looked up to him. The truth was, she had changed the way she thought about him. The fact was, she wanted to sleep with her arms around him tight, to tell him she would always be there for him. But she could tell by the way his face settled into its tough-guy expression that he wouldn't like that.

She wanted to tell him she knew he wasn't Superman. He was flesh and blood and she liked him that way. How much, he would never know. Because all he wanted from her was her respect. Whatever else she might feel had to be concealed.

She lay on her side of the bed, curled up alone, unable to get warm despite the down comforter. She ached to hold him in her arms, to draw warmth and comfort from him as she was eager to give it back.

The next day they both behaved as if the events of the night had never transpired. Matt agreed to meet at the historic mansion for a run-through of the wedding for publicity purposes.

"What should I wear?" he asked when she called him from her office.

"Don't worry. They've got your costume for you."

"That's what I'm worried about. What if it's something I wouldn't be caught dead in?"

"No one you know will ever see you in it. You'll wear it once and that's it."

"I thought you said someone was taking pictures."

"For the Moss Beach weekly. The one we bought the other day. I doubt any of the photos will end up in the *Times*. You have nothing to be afraid of."

Nothing to be afraid of but a crazed gunman waiting for him in L.A. Matt could pretend indifference to the threat, but there was that nightmare. The nightmare he was ignoring. In the morning he'd been his old unflappable, invincible self. So much so she'd wondered if she'd dreamed the whole thing. If she'd only imagined the glimpse into his subconscious that had made her want to shield him from the terrors of the night. Made her want to love him, if he would only let her.

He'd assured her he *wasn't* afraid, just concerned. So concerned he arrived at the rambling, refurnished house ahead of schedule to check out his costume. He had to admit they'd done a good job with the restoration. The floors were polished to their original patina, the beams had been sanded and painted with the same tannin. The wide front porch that had once belonged to the patron looked out onto green fields that stretched all the way to the sea. A nice place for a wedding. Somebody else's wedding.

He saw the costume—a pair of tight pants, a vest and a ruffled shirt. He refused to wear it. Before he wandered out to the front of the house where the photographer was setting up his camera, he hid the whole costume in a butter churn in the kitchen.

"Who're you?" the photographer asked, raising his head from behind the camera.

"I, uh, the groom," Matt mumbled.

"Oh, yeah?" The man looked at Matt's rumpled khakis, the rolled-up sleeves of his oxford cloth shirt and his scuffed deck shoes. "You don't look like a groom."

"I don't feel like one, either."

The photographer's gaze swept up to the second-floor balcony and he whistled through his teeth. "Is that the bride?"

Matt stood transfixed by the sight of Carrie in a vintage white wedding gown. It had been made for some long-lost bride whose family had owned this house, but it fit Carrie as if it had been made for her. The bodice outlined the curve of her breasts, molded her small waist and then flowed to the floor. Her hair was drawn back so that cascades of auburn curls tumbled over one shoulder. She waved to him and he felt all the air whoosh out of his lungs.

"Hi," he called in what was not at all his normal voice. She looked down at him, her eyes soft and velvety, while the photographer snapped picture after picture of her. She could have been the wife of a Spanish land baron, he thought. She could have been the wife of anyone. But she wasn't. Not yet.

He stood there for an eternity, lost in time and place, looking up at her, wondering if they'd met in another life, in the mid-nineteenth century when there was no town, no mayor or chief of police. Just ranchos, an alcalde or maybe a sheriff or two. Would he have swept her off her feet, asked her father for her hand? If he had, would they have drifted apart, just as he and his wife had? Probably, because Matt was not cut out for marriage. He preferred his work. And Carrie deserved better. She would find it, too. The sun made a halo around her body and he wanted to run away with her over the hills to his rancho, despite his rationalizations.

"Hey, you—the groom," called the photographer. "Could you join the bride there on the balcony, but stay in the background?"

Matt clomped up the varnished circular staircase to join Carrie and face the photographer with a forced smile for the camera. Carrie's eyes widened at his clothes, but she didn't say anything. The photographer ordered them to take every imaginable type of pose, carefully keeping Matt behind Carrie so his lack of costume wouldn't show. It was a challenge, but the man let them know he was a professional and he was up to it.

"I'm sorry about this," Carrie said under her breath. "I didn't know it would take so long."

"Neither did I," he said with one arm around her waist, the other holding her hand in his, their bodies wedged together.

"At least you get to wear your own clothes," she murmured. "They've got me buttoned up so tight I can't breathe, and this bra isn't from any museum, it's one of those new models."

Matt glanced down onto the swell of her creamy breasts which appeared to be almost falling out of the décolletage of the white satin dress. "Is that absolutely necessary?" he asked, trying to slow his pounding heart. Every breath she took made him afraid she'd pop out of the dress entirely, and he'd be obliged to shield her from the photographer with his body. The idea left him breathless and he couldn't tear his eyes away.

"That's what they say," Carrie explained with another deep breath that caused him to jerk his eyes away and look at the camera instead.

"No wonder they had such big families," he said, his voice husky. "Husbands couldn't keep their hands off their wives."

"And wives couldn't keep their dresses on," she added. "I wish I were back in uniform," she said, tugging helplessly at her neckline.

"I told you," he teased. "I knew you'd come to your senses."

"You're not listening," the photographer called from the grass below. "You need to move closer, to put your arms around each other."

"Closer?" Matt murmured, wondering how they could *be* any closer. He found out. The smooth satin of the dress was heated by the warmth of her skin and tantalized him to the point of pain. In a few minutes he'd have to excuse himself. He concentrated on the little buttons that marched down the back of her dress and wondered how long it would take him to unbutton them.

All those years seeing Carrie in uniform, behind a bulletproof vest, he'd never known, never thought about what was underneath. Thank God, or he'd never have been able to shoot straight, or even think straight. Right now he didn't have to think. Just go through the motions, follow the photographer's orders. Hold her close, closer. Kiss her. Not like that. Softly. Now deeply. Again. It was torture, pure torture. Did she feel it, too? He couldn't tell.

Matt followed her downstairs. He carried her over the threshold. He stopped. He did it again. The smell of her hair and her skin was driving him wild. He had to get out of there, as far away as he could from this make-believe, this phony fiancé thing.

When the photographer finally let them go, he stumbled across the lawn to the driveway. He hoped Carrie had meant what she'd said about preferring her uniform. Because that meant L.A. Here, as chief of police, they said she could wear whatever she wanted. Even running shoes with her suits. Good for her. Good for them, he thought staring back at the big white house. But too bad for him.

Chapter Seven

A few days later Carrie got her nightgown back, washed and ironed and carefully folded with the little buttons marching up the front in a neat row to the high neckline. When Mandy handed it to her, she gave Carrie a thoughtful look.

"What you need is a bridal shower," she said. "Would you mind if I gave one for you?"

"No. I mean, y-yes," Carrie stammered. "You don't need to do that."

"But I want to. They're loads of fun. All the women come and give you gorgeous lingerie for your trousseau. The kind of stuff you never buy for yourself."

"I know, but I don't think... I mean, it's really kind of you, but..." She already had more lingerie than she would ever need. And if she got any more she would have to give it back when she broke her engagement.

"Besides," Mandy continued, "it will give you a chance to meet some more people. I know they all want to meet you."

"Well, okay, if you're sure..." Carrie sighed and hoped she didn't sound ungrateful.

Mandy smiled and went to the telephone to invite people. There was no way Carrie could stop her without telling her the truth or being rude. At least she had her old nightgown back. Not that she needed it as far as Matt was concerned. He'd taken to staying downstairs talking to their hosts or other guests in the evening until she'd fallen asleep.

It was obvious that he was avoiding her... if you could avoid someone you slept with and ate with and spent every nonworking hour with. What she meant was, he avoided making anything but small talk and didn't touch her except when absolutely necessary. Which was fine with her. It made everything easier. And lonelier. But that was something she just had to get used to.

Things were going well at work. Nobody said anything about Matt not having a job. And they praised Carrie's handling of the drunk at the campground incident. She tried to give credit to Matt, but they wouldn't listen. Then there was the noise abatement warning she issued to the owners of a barking dog. Amusement flickered in Matt's eyes when he heard about that, but what did she care, the town appreciated her. But still no contract. What were they waiting for?

The city council met on Thursdays. It was their usual brown-bag lunch meeting. She heard the rumble of their voices as she passed the closed doors. Maybe this was it. The meeting where they made their decision. She was too nervous to sit at her desk and read a study of criminal rehabilitation. She couldn't concentrate. She walked out the front door and turned right on Main Street wishing Matt were there to have lunch with. To tell her not to worry. But he said he would be too busy. Too busy doing what? She thought he complained there was nothing to do there. So she went to the deli by herself, pausing to greet people along the way, still amazed that she felt more at home here after such a short time than she did in L.A. She sat in the tiny pocket park behind the feed and fuel store to eat her lunch, feeling more and more anxious. If it was still the matter of Matt's job that was standing in her way, she didn't know what she'd do. It wasn't fair to make him come up here and take a job; on the other hand, she understood how they felt.

When she returned to the city hall building, the council was still in a meeting. Carrie fixed herself a cup of instant coffee in the kitchen at the back of the building and walked slowly to her office, pausing at the closed doors to the mayor's office. How could anything take so long? Were they discussing her, or was she just paranoid?

Back in her office she set her coffee on her desk and moved a stack of papers to one side. Under the papers was a huge black spider lying in wait for her. Carrie screamed at the top of her lungs, the sudden jerk of her arm knocking the hot coffee all over her desk, soaking the documents as it ran down onto the carpet. She ran into the hall, her screams dying as members of the council poured out of the mayor's office to gather around her.

"What's wrong?"

"What happened?"

"Are you all right?"

She nodded and wrapped her arms around her waist in an effort to stop shaking. "It was just…just a spider on my desk."

Luke, the mayor's husband, and Joe Rowley, the sanitation commissioner, strode past Carrie and into her office, returning a second later, holding the spider by one leg and dangling it in front of the others. Carrie shuddered and backed away, her eyes round and terrified.

"It's just a toy," Luke explained, twisting the black plastic arachnid in his fingers. "See?"

Carrie nodded, still gasping for air. "I feel really stupid," she confessed in a half whisper.

The mayor put her arm around Carrie. "Don't feel stupid. It's certainly a very realistic toy. I wouldn't like to find it on *my* desk. I wonder who's been playing tricks on you." She looked around at the men on her council. "It's a little early for Halloween."

The men shrugged, but Carrie could tell Her Honor wasn't satisfied. In her no-nonsense voice she called the group back to her office to reconvene the meeting, and Carrie went back to her office to clean up her coffee-soaked desk.

Yes, someone had put the spider there to make Carrie look like a neurotic instead of a capable, levelheaded chief of police. There were a couple of men she suspected didn't want her there. Men who were still holding out for a man. The same men who'd objected the day she'd arrived and whom she'd never been able to win over. But how could she expect them to change their minds so soon? She would have to work harder at being brave. Because this job was worth it.

When Matt came to pick her up that evening and she told him what had happened, he told her she needed a drink. On the open-air terrace of the Sea Breeze restaurant a few miles outside of town, she told him it would take more than a rubber spider to scare her off. As if he didn't know. "I mean, how childish can they be? Thinking a toy spider would make me leave. Who do you think it was?" she asked, stirring her Bloody Mary.

He shook his head. "I thought everyone here loved you."

"Oh, no. You remember the reaction when they found out I wasn't a man. And the hostile questions at the Elks club. I know it's nothing personal. Still, it hurts. They don't want a woman for the job. And they'll do anything they can to keep me from getting it. I guess I didn't realize that until today. First they insist I have a job, then they planted a spider on my desk to see if I'll react like some nervous woman. I did," she said ruefully.

Matt sipped his vodka collins thoughtfully. "Why are you afraid of spiders?"

"I thought I told you. I got bitten once as a child. It wasn't a poisonous spider, but I had an allergic reaction and got all puffed up and itchy."

"No wonder," he said, drawing his eyebrows together in a frown.

"It might never happen again. But I'm careful." She paused. "I'll have to be more careful and less hysterical. I forgot to take a deep breath and practice self-hypnosis."

"You don't really think they'll hold that against you, do you?" Matt looked at her over his glass. "If they do, you don't want to work here."

"They'll come around," she said with more confidence than she felt. "This isn't the only place in the world where women are tested to see if they measure up. And when they don't, like today, you get these I-told-you-so looks. I admit it, I'm afraid of spiders. But does that mean I won't make a good police chief?"

"Of course not," he agreed.

"But you wouldn't have screamed at a spider. Because you aren't afraid of anything."

She looked into his eyes and she remembered his nightmare the night he'd learned someone was trying to kill him. And she knew he remembered, too. He looked away.

"Everyone's afraid of something," he said. "Should we go inside and get something to eat?"

The smell of simmering sauces and meat on a barbecue wafted from the kitchen of the popular seaside restaurant and made her mouth water.

"I can't. Mandy's bridal shower is tonight."

"What?"

"Didn't I tell you she's giving me a shower?" He looked puzzled, so Carrie explained. "A bunch of women get together and give presents like lingerie and things for your... honeymoon. It's so embarrassing. Especially since

I'm not getting married and I'll have to return everything. And everyone makes jokes about your wedding night..."

She fought off a wave of heat that threatened to engulf her. Talk about embarrassment. Why did she feel it was her duty to explain a bridal shower? "Mandy's been so sweet," she continued. "She wants me to meet people. I couldn't turn her down. I just wish..." She trailed off, avoiding his gaze. He had this way of looking at her lately, with questions in his eyes, the questions he wanted to ask, but couldn't.

"Wish you were really getting married?" he asked.

"Of course not," she said firmly. "Not any more than you do. We've hashed this all out before. I haven't found anyone to marry and I doubt I ever will. What about you?"

"No," he said, laying some money on the table for the waiter. "Once is enough."

As they walked across the patio, she snuck a look at him out of the corner of her eye. "What went wrong?" she asked.

He let out an exasperated sigh and she was instantly sorry she'd asked. "You want to know what went wrong? I'll tell you. Nothing went wrong. Nothing went right, either. I was wrapped up in my work, as usual. I didn't want to bring it home with me because it's depressing. You know that. So we had nothing to talk about."

They got into his car. Matt crossed his arms on the steering wheel and sat there without moving or speaking. After a long moment, Carrie wondered if he remembered she was even there or what they'd been talking about. She held her breath, hoping he'd go on, realizing this was a rare moment.

"The problem was," he continued at last, "I had no idea what a happy marriage was supposed to be like. I blamed it on my parents, or lack of parents. But I know now it was my fault. We drifted apart and I just let it happen." He glanced at her. "I know. You don't believe me. You think that can't be it. There must be something else, something more. Nobody would let his marriage collapse for no reason at all. But that's what happened." He didn't give Carrie a chance to say anything. He went on as if now that he'd broken his silence surrounding his divorce, he was determined to get it all out at once. "It's hard to believe, but there was no reason for our marriage to end. But there was no reason for it to continue, either. I didn't hate her. She didn't hate me.

"But we didn't love each other, either. So I let it slide away, slip through my fingers." He let his head fall forward and rest on his arms.

"I understand," she said softly.

"You do? I don't. Was it my job that made us fall out of love? Was it her or was it me? It left me feeling helpless. And it's not a feeling I enjoy."

She nodded. "You always know what to do."

"I used to." He roused himself, started the car and slowly drove to the inn in the gathering dusk.

Carrie felt guilt wash over her. By taking Matt away from his routine she'd made him look at his life with the perspective of time and distance. It had made him restless and uneasy and he didn't know what to do about it. His usual certainty had been shaken. He might be secretly attracted to this way of life, even more secretly attracted to her, but he didn't know what to do about either. So he was going to do nothing. Nothing at all.

"Look," she said when he stopped the car in front of the big brown house and they both got out. "You've done all you can for me. Why don't you go home? I'll manage on my own. They have to get used to the idea sometime. It might as well be now."

He rocked back on his heels. "What, before you've got the job locked up? I don't think that's such a good idea. We've come this far. I'm not going to quit on you now." He moved his head to one side to look into the lit living room.

"Good God, the place is crawling with women. I'm outta here." He looked down at her, his eyes suddenly brimming with amusement. "But first let's give them something to talk about."

The combination of good humor and sexual awareness in his voice caught her by surprise. It was a welcome change from the despair and uncertainty of only a few minutes ago. And she had to encourage it. She licked her dry lips and tried to calm her beating heart. It's just for show, she told herself as he ran his hands down her arms, then pulled her to him.

Her lips met his, more than halfway. She wanted, *needed* his kisses, his warmth and his strength. All the frustrations of the day melted away with the heat of his mouth on hers, his tongue parting her lips and seeking, delving, wanting her as much as she wanted him. She knotted her hands around his neck and tilted her face so he could trail kisses down her face to her throat. She staggered backward, he went with her.

She wanted him to lift her up in his arms so she could wrap her legs around him. "Matt," she murmured.

"What do you want me to do?" His breath was warm against her ear. The ocean breeze, cool only a few minutes ago, was now hot and heavy against her fevered brow.

"Take me away from all this," she said.

He groaned, a deep sound that came from his chest and reverberated throughout her body. "You don't mean it."

"No," she whispered. "I have to go, but I...don't... want to."

Carrie could have stayed there all night, matching kiss for kiss, sigh for sigh, until he'd carried her into the house and up the stairs. If it hadn't been for the shower... If it hadn't been for the shower he wouldn't have been compelled to put on a show. It was all a show.

The front door opened and feminine laughter spilled out into the twilight. "Carrie ... we're waiting for you," they called.

She pulled away from Matt and tucked her blouse into her skirt with shaky hands.

"Do you think they got their money's worth?" he asked.

"I don't know about them," she said, smoothing her hair, "but I did." She could have sworn he, too, felt something more than satisfaction in fooling a bunch of women. She just didn't know how much. She wiped her damp palms against her skirt and swallowed hard. "Thanks," she breathed. "If I don't get this job, it won't be your fault."

He let out a long breath. "Anytime," he said with a studied casual tone. His eyes lingered on the errant curls that clung to her temples, the bright spots of color that stained her cheekbones. Then he watched her turn and walk unsteadily toward the house. And he knew the game was up.

He could no longer pretend to help her while sabotaging her behind her back. He wanted her, yes, as his partner back in L.A. but that wasn't going to happen. She belonged here. He knew that, he'd known it since they'd first set foot in the town. He just didn't want to admit it. He leaned against the car, his back to the house, and thought about how dismal it would feel to go back without her. But that wasn't the issue.

She didn't want to go back. He did. She wanted to stay here. He didn't. He understood. Almost understood. She wouldn't mind the long boring evenings where nothing happened. Maybe she would get married. She hadn't said she wouldn't. In a white satin dress in a historic mansion. He ground his teeth. Not to someone else. To some boring guy with a boring job? No way. Is that what she really wanted? She wouldn't be happy. She would come running back to L.A., to him, admitting he was right. He smiled to himself as he pictured her flinging herself into his arms, her body meshed perfectly with his, the smell of honey and almonds overwhelming his senses, bringing back memories...

They would return to their old office, to their old beat. But what about everything that had happened here? Could he ever forget how she felt in his arms, how she tasted, how she looked in silk and satin? How she slept with one arm around her pillow...without wanting more than partnership? Could he ever stop replaying that scene in the bedroom when he'd first stepped over the boundary into lotusland? When he'd realized Carrie was more than his partner? She was a desirable woman, soft, sweet, warm...

After a dinner of yogurt on Main Street he walked down the quiet street to the corner where the deserted saloon stood. The double doors were hand-carved, weather-beaten, but still solid. He peered through the dirt-streaked window until his eyes got used to the dark and he could see chairs stacked upside down on top of tables. It might work. There was enough space for a small group of musicians. If that's what people wanted.

He looked up and down the street. Who knew what the people here wanted? If he built it, would anyone come? Did it matter? He wasn't going to open a coffeehouse in Moss Beach, California. Even if there was no place to get a decent cup of cappuccino around here, not to mention espresso, *latte*... He wasn't going to open a coffeehouse anywhere. He wasn't the entrepreneurial type. But if he did open one, this wouldn't be a bad spot, he thought, pressing his forehead against the window.

He killed some more time by rearranging the bar in his mind, until it had become a coffeehouse with ferns hanging from the ceiling and huge apothecary jars filled with coffee beans on the shelves. When he finally went back to the inn, he was glad to see the women had left.

Carrie and Mandy were alone in the living room, surrounded by boxes and ribbons and empty plates and coffee cups and long-stemmed champagne glasses.

He opened the front door and angled his head into the room. "All done?" he inquired lightly.

Carrie jumped, then covered the box she'd been looking at. "All done," she said. "Mandy gave the most fabulous party."

"Everyone loves Carrie," Mandy said from her reclining position on the couch. "You should see the stuff she got. You *will* see it," she said gleefully. "Go ahead, Carrie, go on upstairs with Matt. I'll clean up."

"No, you won't." Carrie got to her feet. "You go to bed, Mandy," she insisted. "I'll clean up here."

Matt looked from Carrie to their pregnant hostess. "*I'll* clean up," he decided. "You both look tired. What did you do, anyway?"

"We talked and laughed and toasted the bride with champagne," Mandy explained. She yawned. "Maybe I will go to bed. Just leave everything. I'll do it in the morning."

Carrie nodded, but after Mandy left the room she and Matt took all the dirty dishes into the kitchen. Matt glanced at Carrie, noticing that her eyes were drooping. He grasped her firmly by her shoulders and pushed her gently into a kitchen chair. "Sit down," he said firmly. "You're dead on your feet." He proceeded to load the dishwasher while she watched through glazed eyes.

"It's the pretending," she said softly. "It takes a lot out of you."

As if he didn't know. "You mean pretending you're really getting married. That you need all that . . . stuff."

"Yes. They're all so *happy* for me. My mouth hurts from smiling." She looked up at him and gave him a helpless half smile. "See?"

He saw the strain in the lines in her forehead, in the way she held her chin up in her hand. He wished he could do something for her.

"I just kept thinking of having to give everything back, of explaining why we called it off. How have things gotten so far out of hand?" she asked, wrinkling her nose.

"They'll understand, won't they?" he asked, bracing his hand against the kitchen counter. He wanted to cup her face in his hands, kiss her troubles away, get lost in those dark, dreamy eyes....

"I suppose so." She sighed. "What was it I'd decided to say?" She passed her hand across her forehead. "I can't think."

For the life of him Matt couldn't remember what the reason was for their breaking their nonexistent engagement. Right there at that moment, in that big, comfortable kitchen, he couldn't think of a single reason why they shouldn't get married and live happily ever after right here in Moss Beach. He knew there *were* reasons, good reasons, but he couldn't bring them to mind. Not with her looking at him like that, her red hair in disarray around her freckled face, her hand against her cheek, her eyes soft and luminous.

He could offer to marry her. But what was the point? It wouldn't work. She was so naive she probably thought all it took was love. He knew better. It took something else, something he didn't have. So it was better to break an engagement than a marriage. It had to be.

He wanted the best for Carrie. And now he knew the best was not returning to L.A. with him. It was staying here as chief of police. The realization hit him like a kitchen knife in the gut. So now came the real challenge. First, he'd had to pretend to be in love with her. Now he'd have to pretend *not* to be in love with her.

"All you have to do," he said, "is explain that we're incompatible. We don't want the same things." Except for each other. They wanted each other.

"That's right," she said sleepily. "You miss the city. The danger and excitement. You can hardly wait to get back."

He nodded. "And I think I've solved the employment problem. If they want me to have a job, I'll get one. I'll open a coffeehouse on Main Street."

"What? When did this happen?"

"It was Adam's idea," he explained. "As you know, there's a dearth of good coffee in this town. And no entertainment. And there's an empty store on Main Street. I just have to find the owner, give him a month's rent, go through the motions. Hopefully word will spread, and you'll have your job."

Carrie's head spun. She didn't understand. She shouldn't have had two glasses of champagne, not on top of a drink with Matt on top of no dinner.

The kitchen door opened and Adam looked in at them. "What's happening?" he asked.

Carrie got to her feet unsteadily, the champagne and the emotions combining to bring her to a state of exhaustion. "Matt's got some good news. I'm going to bed." She brushed past Adam before Matt could stop her.

She gathered up her boxes in the living room and staggered up the stairs. She may be tired and a little bit drunk, but she still realized what had happened. Matt had decided to let her go. He no longer wanted her to return with him. Up until now Carrie had suspected he'd secretly sabotaged her efforts to get the job. And secretly she was a little flattered to think he wanted her to come back that badly.

But he'd changed his mind. By going through the motions to open a coffeehouse, he would be doing all he could to make sure she got the job. She would never see him again. She dragged her feet up the steps, fighting off tears of disappointment and fatigue. She told herself she was

getting what she wanted. She should be celebrating instead
of crying. But it didn't do any good. She headed for the
bathroom and drew a hot bath where she could drown her
sorrows.

As the hot water gushed into the deep, white porcelain
claw-foot tub, Carrie undressed and held up one of the
gifts, a pale pink silk teddy edged with lace around the
bodice and the bottom. Through the steam she looked at
herself in the bathroom mirror, wishing she had the nerve
to wear such an outrageously sexy garment. But she wasn't
the type. She was the granny-gown type. And she had no
one to wear it for anyway. She wasn't engaged. She wasn't
getting married. It was bad enough wearing that green silk
negligee Matt had given her, knowing it was for Mandy's
benefit and not Matt's.

On the other hand, she thought, hanging the teddy on a
hook on the bathroom door, maybe this was her one chance
to wear it. Her last chance. Technically they had five days
left, but the minute they offered her the job, she suspected
Matt would be gone. This was her opportunity to show him
what he'd be missing. She added an extra dash of bubble
bath to the water and slid into the tub, resting her head on
the rim.

"Carrie?"

At the sound of Matt's voice just outside the bathroom
door Carrie slid even further into the water until it lapped
at her chin. "Yes?"

"I brought you another glass of champagne. Do you
want it in there?"

Carrie looked at the wide expanse of pink bubbles cov-
ering her body and shrugged. She didn't *need* any more
champagne, but why not?

"Sure." She was about to lift herself out of the tub to
unlock the door when she realized she'd never locked it.

The door opened slowly and Matt eased his way into the
room, his eyes wary but wide open. She held out her hand

and took the glass, letting his hand brush against hers, sending a tingling sensation up her arm in the direction of her heart. "Bubbles," she noted, holding the glass up to the light. "I'm surrounded by bubbles." Then a small giggle escaped unbidden from her lips.

"Carrie." Matt took a step backward. "Are you drunk?"

She took a sip of the champagne and peered at him over the rim of the glass. "I don't know. How can you tell?"

"Well . . ." He leaned back against the door. "All your feelings are intensified. If you feel happy, you're happier, and so forth."

She set her glass carefully on the edge of the tub and licked her lips. "I feel very silly. Like laughing and crying all at once," she said, avoiding his gaze. "Could that be it?"

"It could. Maybe I ought to take that back." He bent to retrieve the glass, but she reached for his arm with her wet hand to stop him. At the same time her body floated to the top of the water and her rosy pink nipples peeked through the bubbles.

Matt drew in a sharp breath at the tantalizing sight. "I'd better get out of here," he muttered.

"Why? You just got here," she noted, playfully blowing a bubble in his direction.

"You're not yourself," he said, his eyes riveted to the places on her body where the bubbles were fast disappearing.

"Hmm-mmm." She sank back under the water, and he exhaled slowly, feeling like he'd just run up a flight of stairs. "It's funny," she mused. "A little while ago I was so sad, so terribly sad, and now...I'm not." She smiled up at him, a silly, giddy smile he'd never seen before. But he didn't return her smile. He couldn't. Not with his throat so tight he couldn't swallow.

"Why don't you have some champagne, Matt? I guarantee you'll forget all your troubles. I can't even remember what mine were." She shrugged lightly, which caused the foam to cascade over her creamy breasts and settle on the rosy buds that puckered and pouted for his benefit.

Fascinated, he watched the waves lap against her tummy, and all of a sudden he couldn't breathe. The urge to reach out and touch was almost overwhelming. His head was so heavy he thought he might pass out. It must be the heat and the steam and the sight of a totally naked, totally perfect Carrie Stephens. He groped for the doorknob but he couldn't find it.

"Do you think you could do me a favor?" she asked before he could find his way out.

"Sure." Was that his voice or the sound of gravel scraping against asphalt?

"Scrub my back? I can't reach it. I can't reach anything," she said, looking up at him from under red-gold lashes.

He shouldn't scrub her back. He shouldn't do anything but get the hell out of there. But without thinking, he kneeled on the floor. He picked up a sponge from the shelf by the tub and immersed it in the water. She leaned forward. He lifted her red curls from the back of her neck with one hand and with the other began to massage her shoulders with the sponge.

"That feels . . . so . . . good," she said softly. "You can't imagine."

He *could* imagine. He could imagine that and a whole lot more. Like lifting her out of that tub, toweling her off with soft terry cloth, touching her where he wanted, where *she* wanted. Then letting his lips follow. He could almost taste her skin. Like fresh flowers, soft as petals. If she thought the back massage felt good . . .

His mouth went dry despite the steam in the room. He wanted her. There was no more denying it. He wanted her in the most elemental way. Right here and now. And she wasn't doing anything to discourage him. In fact, if she weren't drunk, he would accuse her of seducing him. But she didn't want him. Not really. She wanted the job.

She'd made that perfectly clear. Over and over. Oh, sometimes she looked at him with admiration when she thought he didn't notice. But that was for Matt the tough cop, her partner. She might even have had a crush on him at the beginning. But by now she knew better. Knew that he wasn't going to get involved with anybody. Especially not his partner.

But who'd said anything about involvement? All he wanted to do was what was best for Carrie, then cut out.

She looked up at him, her dark brown eyes dreamy, her mouth curved in a sensuous smile. "Don't go," she said.

"I have to go."

"But I might drown," she teased, and dipped her head back under the water until her hair streamed out around her face.

"Carrie," he begged, staggering backward, aching to kiss her on all her most sensitive spots, most of which he could now see in the fast-disappearing bubbles. With a superhuman effort, he turned the doorknob at last. "I'm going now."

"Good," she said, bumping her head on the porcelain and gazing up at him. "Go get some more champagne."

"No more champagne," he said as he closed the door firmly behind him. "Not for you." But he filled his own glass and sat on the edge of the bed, letting the night air blow in the window and cool his fevered face. He looked across the room at the mirror over the bureau. "She's drunk," he muttered. "What's your excuse?"

"Don't say it's love," the man in the mirror cautioned. "You don't know the meaning of the word. You're confusing it with lust."

"What did you say?" Carrie called from the bathroom.

"Nothing. Just trying to figure something out."

The bathroom door opened and Carrie came out dressed in a pale pink teddy, so sheer she might as well be wearing nothing at all. He supposed this was the idea. But, good grief, how was he supposed to control himself?

"Can I help?" Carrie asked, one hand on her hip, the other holding her glass of champagne, an innocent imitation of a seasoned seductress.

He closed his eyes, buried his head in his hands and groaned.

Chapter Eight

With shaking hands, Carrie set her empty glass on the dresser and rushed to Matt's side. "What's wrong?" she asked, kneeling beside him. "Are you okay?"

Capturing his face between her hands, she lifted his head to face her. But he wouldn't look at her. "It's the lights," he said. "They're so bright."

"I'm sorry." She scrambled across the room and turned off the lamps on the dresser, then flipped the wall switch until all that was left was a pale shaft of light from the moon breaking through the fog outside the window. "Better?" she asked. She knew how he felt. The lights had hurt her eyes and the room was spinning around. Maybe if she held on to him, if they held on to each other, it would stop. She got onto the bed and sat cross-legged behind him, pressing herself against his back.

If only he weren't wearing that heavy oxford cloth shirt that was such a barrier between them. She reached around to fumble with the buttons with both hands, but fumble was all she could do.

"What are you doing?" he demanded, capturing her hands in his.

"Just trying to help you," she explained. What was wrong with him? Didn't he know how good it felt to shed your clothes and discard your inhibitions? She'd never felt so light, so free, so... so tired. She closed her eyes and her head fell forward, her cheek pressed against the sturdy cotton of his shirt, unable to get any closer.

Then she was falling backward, down, down, down onto a big, white, fluffy cloud. She couldn't see it, but she could feel it. She felt something else, too. Someone lifting her with strong arms, smoothing her cheek with gentle hands, laying her down and holding her as tightly as she'd held him, with her back tucked into his chest, their legs jack-knifed. And she slept, blissfully, deeply, until she woke up in the morning with a pounding headache and Matt's arms wound around her.

With only a hasty glance at his disheveled hair and bare, muscular torso, she slid out of his arms without waking him and went to the bathroom to swallow a pain reliever. The image in the mirror wasn't promising. To her horror she was wearing the sheerest, sexiest garment she'd received last night at the shower. She might as well have been wearing nothing at all. And then to top it off, she'd gotten drunk. Or was she drunk when she'd put on the teddy?

Bits and pieces of the preceding night filtered through to her aching brain. The more she remembered, the worse she felt. She'd practically seduced Matt. The only reason she hadn't succeeded was either that he didn't want to be seduced or she'd fallen asleep before she'd done it. The last thing she remembered was trying to undress him. The face in the mirror turned crimson as the memories flooded back. She scrubbed her face vigorously with the French-milled soap, trying to make the shame disappear. There was a knock on the bathroom door and the soap slid out of her hands and onto the floor.

"You okay?" he asked hoarsely.

She opened the door a crack. His hair stood on end, his face was shadowed with a rough stubble. She held out her hand as if to run her fingers around his jaw to see how it felt, then snatched it back. "Fine," she said, allowing her gaze to wander down his chest to where the dark hair disappeared beneath the waistband of his plaid boxers. She jerked her eyes back to his. "How about you?"

"Yes."

She wanted to ask so many questions, but she didn't dare. He stared at her as if he wondered if it was a dream. Maybe it was. Who would believe that Carrie Stephens would drink too much champagne and try to seduce her partner? And fail. It wasn't possible, except for the last part. Face it, she could dance naked in the room and he still wouldn't want her. She almost had, and he hadn't. A new pain had settled in the region of her heart to compete with the throbbing in her head.

"Well..." Carrie picked up her toothbrush and looked pointedly at the toothpaste, and Matt closed the door. When she came out, he was gone. She dressed quickly, in a navy blue lightweight wool dress and those stupid walking shoes. She wanted her other shoes back. The ones that were in the trunk of his car. The ones that matched her dress. But she couldn't ask him for them. It was too late. It had gone beyond that. She also wanted her head back, the one that used to be attached to her shoulders but now floated somewhere above it, pounding incessantly.

She hurried down the stairs to find Matt standing at the door talking to Mandy. She heard snatches of the conversation. "A great idea...the whole town...just what we need." To her disgust Matt looked rested, well-shaven, combed, and unbelievably sexy for that early in the morning.

She said good morning to Mandy then turned to Matt. "You don't have to drive me to work," she said.

"I want to," he answered, guiding her out the door with the slightest pressure from his hand on the small of her back. "I told Mandy we'd have breakfast in town. She looked almost as tired as you."

"Is that how I look?" she asked, getting into the car.

"You look good considering..." He shot her an appreciative glance as he backed out of Mandy's driveway.

"Considering what? Go ahead, tell me. I made a fool of myself last night, didn't I?"

He couldn't conceal the smile that tugged at the corners of his wide, generous mouth. "I wouldn't say that."

"What would you say?" she demanded, fastening her seat belt with a vigorous snap.

"I'd say you showed a different side of yourself."

"I'd say I showed a whole lot more than that." She turned her face to the window and looked with intense interest at the sea oats that grew in the sandy soil along the road.

"It was just between you and me, you know," he said quietly. "Nobody else knows what happened."

"But they'll imagine," she said. "You should have heard the remarks as I opened the presents."

"Does that bother you?" he asked, his voice oddly serious. He stopped the car and looked at her.

"What bothers me is that I came on to you..." She stared straight ahead, unwilling to look him in the eye. "And you..."

"I put you to bed."

"Yes. I threw myself at you... and you..."

"Threw you right back. Is that what you think?" He touched the curve of her cheek with his knuckles so gently she felt close to tears.

"Didn't you?" she asked, finally meeting his level gaze.

"When we make love," he said, taking her hands in his, "I want you to know exactly what you're doing. I want you to want me as much as I want you. I want both of us to be wide awake, and I want you to wear that . . . thing you were wearing. So that I can take it off you, slowly, or maybe fast . . ." Matt's voice, so intense, finally tapered off as it clogged with emotion. The heat from his gaze burned its way to her core. She twisted her fingers away from his and tried to catch her breath.

He said "when" they made love, not "if." He said he wanted her. And God knows she wanted him. But it wasn't going to happen. Time was running out. He would be gone soon. But before he left, he was trying to rebuild her tattered ego. So she wouldn't feel like a fool or a failure.

She managed to give him a quavery smile. If she could speak she would thank him for his kind, reassuring words. But all she could do was to look at her watch. Matt got the hint. He drove her to town without speaking. They ate breakfast at the coffee shop on Main Street.

"See that building across the street?" he asked, establishing with his casual tone that they were back to being friends.

She glanced over her shoulder. "The one on the corner with the For Rent sign in the window?"

"Do you think it would make a good coffeehouse?"

"Looks like it needs some work," she said, referring to the peeling paint on the trim, the empty flower boxes and the dirty windows.

"Well, of course," he said, "or it wouldn't be a challenge." He watched as a man appeared in front of the shop and opened the front door.

"Uh-oh," Carrie said. "It looks like somebody beat you to it."

He stood, leaving half of his omelet and hash brown potatoes on his plate. "Excuse me," he said. "I've got to check this out."

Carrie watched him jog across the street, knock on the door of the shop and disappear inside. He was certainly throwing himself into this idea of fooling the town. He was so good at it he'd almost fooled her, too. She wished she could enjoy it half as much as he did. But it made her feel sad to know she was pulling the wool over the eyes of a whole town, that they were being tricked into hiring her.

Not that she wouldn't do a good job. Not that she wasn't right for the job. It was just too bad she'd had to resort to this trickery to convince them. She sighed, paid the check, and walked to work, noting that Matt had never emerged from the shop.

She didn't see him for another hour when he marched into city hall and asked the license department in an office down the hall from hers for a permit to operate a business. Shamelessly she stood outside the office listening to his conversation. She saw him filling out forms, and when he looked up and saw her, he gave her a conspiratorial wink. She wanted to ask how he'd managed it, but it could wait until later. She hoped he hadn't had to put down any money. She hoped he could get out of town without being lynched.

A short time later, after he'd left the building, the whole place was abuzz with the news that Carrie's fiancé was going to open a coffeehouse on Main Street, with live music on weekends. Carrie closed the door to her office, trying not to imagine the disappointment when they found out it wasn't true. She stayed there until the mayor called her into her office.

"I told you it would happen," Mayor Thompson said with a delighted smile. "The job is yours. No one has any further objections. I couldn't be happier. I think you and Lt. Graham will be an outstanding addition to our community."

Carrie managed to force a smile. She hated to think of facing the mayor in a few short days telling her the whole thing had fallen through—the marriage, the coffeehouse, everything. But Carrie signed her contract, which provided her with generous health benefits, the rent-free house with option to buy, and a retirement package that she would be eligible for in twenty years.

Twenty years stretched ahead of her like a lonely winding road. Would she ever find someone to travel that road with her? Or would she grow old alone, patrolling Main Street, investigating stolen hubcaps from the parking lot at the beach and attending potluck dinners all by herself?

Before Carrie left the mayor's office, the mayor said, "Luke and I would like to invite you and your fiancé to dinner tonight at the Sea Breeze. Did you know it was once a hideout for smugglers? It's supposed to be haunted, as well. Anyway, I want to celebrate. If you're free."

If they were free? What else could they possibly have to do? Maybe Matt was right, maybe she would feel isolated here, trapped and bored. "We'd love to," she assured her boss and headed back to her office, where she let her head fall forward onto a stack of documents she was planning to read. Her head was too heavy to hold up anymore. The pounding had ceased, replaced by an achy tiredness.

All she wanted to do was go back to bed, to sleep for days and wake up when it was all over. When Matt was gone and everyone knew he wasn't coming back. But then she would have to endure pitying looks and knowing glances, or at the very least, a reproachful silence. No, there wasn't a whole lot to look forward to, she admitted.

There was a knock on the door. She lifted her head and shuffled some papers, trying to look busy. But it was only Matt, looking energized and alert and busy. Which only made her feel worse.

"Look what I've got," he said, holding up a signed agreement with the owner of the old saloon.

"Was that really necessary?" she asked with a frown. "Couldn't you have just *said* you were going to do it?"

He shook his head. "It had to be real. But don't worry. It has an escape clause."

An escape clause. How appropriate. Matt had made sure he could get away from her, from the town and from his agreement. She felt an unbecoming twinge of resentment.

"And I've got a lead on a band."

"What?" Now he'd gone too far.

"They're high school students. I'm going to hire them for one night only. Tomorrow night. We'll give the town a taste of music and some real coffee—if I can get my hands on some—and see what happens. It'll be like a grand opening."

"And a closing, all in one night," she said, not even trying to hide the disapproval in her voice.

"Nobody needs to know that," he said with a smile that told her he hadn't noticed her lack of enthusiasm. That he hadn't given a thought to what would happen when he left, when she would have to answer the questions, to pick up the pieces. "Spread the word," he said, walking to the window and looking out at the trees that lined the sidewalk. "I want the whole town there."

Carrie nodded. Matt sounded like he'd just booked the Beatles to sing on the *Ed Sullivan Show* and wanted to be sure everyone tuned in. "I've got something to show you," she said, feeling slightly overshadowed. She held up the contract she'd just signed.

He crossed the room and snatched it out of her hand and read it sitting on the edge of her desk. "You did it," he said at last. "Congratulations." He held out his hand and took hers. Without breaking eye contact he held her hand for a long time. If she stayed in Moss Beach for another twenty years she would never forget the look in his eyes, as if he'd connected to the very depths of her soul and he knew everything, how she felt about his leaving and her staying. She tried to look away, to hide her feelings, but his gaze held hers until the town clock chimed twelve noon.

She pulled her hand away. She didn't want him to know. Didn't want him to care. To feel sorry for her. "Well," she said briskly, getting up from behind her desk. "How about lunch?"

"Sorry," he said, easing off her desk. "I've got things to do and people to see."

"Okay." She watched him walk out of her office, feeling like she'd just lost her best friend. She had. Lost him to an imaginary coffeehouse and ultimately to his real life six hundred miles away. She followed him to the front of the building. "We're invited to dinner tonight with the mayor and her husband, at the Sea Breeze."

He nodded and then he was gone, disappearing around the corner of city hall on his way back to Main Street.

Matt let himself into the building with his key. It was a good location. Right in the heart of town. A good place for people to see their friends and hang out over a *good* cup of coffee. He looked around at the walls and the windows, realizing just how much needed to be done. If he'd known that Carrie had had her contract, would he have gone this far? He looked at the old bar and he knew he wanted to see it polished and used again, lined with customers drinking Java—and Blue Mountain. It might be crazy, but it was his last chance at craziness. After this, it was back to real life.

And it gave him something to do. All afternoon he scrubbed and washed and polished. While he did, he worried about what would happen when he left. He hoped the townspeople wouldn't take it out on Carrie. They would feel sorry for her, that was for sure. Being deserted by that dirtbag, that rotten fiancé of hers.

They might be extra nice to her. Take her under their collective wing. Invite her out. Fix her up with eligible men. He stifled a groan of protest, setting his broom down and going to look out the window. If he turned his head, he could just see the roof of her house. The house she loved. She would be happy here, he knew it, and he would have the satisfaction of knowing he'd helped make it possible.

* * *

That evening Matt and Carrie met the mayor and her husband at their house in the Lago del Mar subdivision located just outside town. It was clear that Luke had had a change of heart since their first meeting when he'd objected to Carrie being a woman. He congratulated her, apologized on behalf of the town for the spider incident, and took her arm to escort her to their car for the drive to the restaurant.

Carrie and Matt sat in the back seat. He reached for her hand and laced her fingers through his. He was proud of her for winning over her most vociferous critics. She gave him a glance that told him she considered this dinner an ordeal. He could tell by the tiny frown lines that deepened her forehead. He wanted her to relax. It was almost over. He put her hand on his thigh and she gave a tiny, almost imperceptible gasp as her warm hand connected with the muscle in his leg.

He heard Carrie converse with the mayor and her husband about moving into her house, but he couldn't make sense of it. His thoughts kept returning to the scene in the bathroom last night. Wondering if it would ever happen again. Wondering how he could make it happen again, with a different ending. No, he couldn't do that. No matter how much he loved her.

Not love, lust. There was a big difference. Love was something that lasted forever. Something he didn't understand and wasn't capable of. He realized there was silence in the car. All eyes were on him, waiting for him to say something.

"They were wondering how many people you want to invite to the wedding," Carrie prompted.

"I'll make a list," he promised. He'd forgotten about the wedding. The costume with the ruffles and the tight collar that he was never going to wear. But he could see the others hadn't. They were talking about the caterers, the tents set up outside and the coffee.

"You'll see to ordering the coffee, won't you, Matt?" the mayor asked with a twinkle in her eye. "We'll want the very best, you know, for our mayor and for our sesquicentennial."

"We have some time, don't we?" Matt asked. They weren't going to squeeze it in before he left, were they?

The mayor laughed. "Of course. We're planning it for October, when our weather is at its best. I hope that gives you enough time."

Matt managed a smile and Carrie nodded, and he hoped the subject was closed.

Once inside the restaurant and seated at a table by the window with a view of the giant rocks that jutted out into the sea, Luke told the story of the famous ghost that haunted the old building. "In the days of the smugglers, that is to say, the late eighteen hundreds, there was a woman who lived here."

"This was just a house at the time," Margaret added.

"She used to wait for her lover, a pirate and a smuggler, every night, holding a lit candle in the window so he could see his way to shore to leave off his bounty."

"Are you sure it was a candle, Luke?" his wife interjected.

"Well, it wasn't a flashlight. Can I go on?" he asked. She nodded and he continued. "Folks say she'd go down to the beach by night to pick up the bounty to hide it for him until he came for it and her. Then one night he finally came ashore and they were waiting for him."

"The police?" chorused Matt and Carrie together.

"No police in those days."

"Customs? Immigration?" Matt asked.

"Just a sheriff," Luke said, "and his deputies. Well, the woman leaned out the window, shot the sheriff, and sailed away with her lover, but not the goods."

"Then who's the ghost?" asked Carrie.

"The dead sheriff. His deputies fled, leaving his body on the beach. When they went back the next day, it was gone. They say he haunts the place, looking for the lost treasure. He comes up to the house and rattles around. They say he won't leave until he finds it."

"Sounds like an officer of the law," Matt said, "tenacious to the end. And beyond." He looked around the dining room at the candles on the white linen tablecloths, which reminded him of their first dinner here in town. He smiled into Carrie's eyes, wondering if she remembered, too. When she nudged his knee with her stockinged foot, he knew she did.

While the mayor and her husband argued about which was best, the sole or the halibut, Matt reached under the table and took her bare ankle, encircling it with his thumb and forefinger. He carefully put her foot in his lap, against his thigh.

Her lips parted, her eyes darkened, and she gripped her fork tightly. Fortunately Luke and Margaret were still so engaged in conversation they didn't notice that their new chief of police was being seduced during the salad course. And if they had, they might have written it off to young love. Love. Matt winced. That word again. Carrie pulled her foot away and concentrated on her salad.

The meal seemed to go on and on. When would it end? Matt wondered. When could they go back to their room? And what would happen when they did? He was faced with a serious decision. Carrie wanted him, her eyes told him so, as did the look on her face and the flush that tinted her face to a rosy pink. And he wanted her. No doubt about that. He wanted her in a way he'd never wanted anyone.

But Carrie wanted a husband. She deserved a husband. And he had to get away from here. To get back to work, back to normal. Whatever that was. He could hold out for a few more days, though. He had to.

After an eternity, after they'd gone back to the mayor's house and begged off a nightcap, they finally arrived back at the inn. Before they got out of the car, Matt turned to Carrie.

"What are you going to tell people after I leave?" he asked.

She leaned against the passenger door and studied his profile. He could feel her eyes on him, but he looked straight ahead.

"I don't know," she confessed. "I don't want to think about it. But don't worry, I'll think of something."

"How about, I've come down with something, something I don't want to burden you with. A mysterious disease."

"So who would take care of you? They'd think I was heartless if I let you wander off to suffer on your own. I couldn't let you do it."

She was right. She was too good, too kind to let anybody go off and suffer. He racked his brain to come up with another topic for discussion. Anything to prolong the moment of truth when they faced each other again in that room, both of them cold sober tonight, with their wits about them.

"This is a big day for you," he remarked.

"For you, too," she said.

"You're not nervous, are you?" he asked, noticing she was perched on the edge of the bucket seat as if poised to take off.

"About the job? No."

He wanted to ask if there was anything *else* she was nervous about, like what was next for them.

"I have you to thank. For giving up your vacation. And then playing your part so well. You deserve an award, the Academy Award, at least."

"It wasn't that hard." Not hard at all to pretend to be in love with her. "You were the star. I was just a supporting player."

"I don't know how to be a star," she said, looking away.

"Get used to it," he said. "Pretty soon you'll have the whole town at your feet." He looked at her feet and he knew this was the time to give her back her shoes, to confess what he'd been up to all along. But then he would have to explain why he'd changed his mind. He didn't want her to think it had anything to do with his feelings for her. The way he wanted the best for her made it sound like... something like love. So he let the moment pass.

The silence between them grew. She was obviously as reluctant as he was to go into the house. The memory of her in that pale pink thing she'd worn kept intruding on his thoughts. He was desperate for something to say.

"It wasn't all acting, you know," he said at last. "I mean, you're an attractive woman, you know that. So it wasn't hard to act like... like..." Oh, God, the more he said, the worse it got. She didn't want flattery; she didn't deserve it. She deserved the truth.

"The truth is I'm... I think you're really...special," he said, knowing it was the understatement of the year. But he wasn't about to tell her she was the loveliest, the sexiest, the most intriguing woman he'd ever known, that her hair reminded him of shiny new pennies, and that it took every ounce of willpower he had to keep his hands off of her. And that when his willpower failed... "I don't know why I never noticed you before, I mean, noticed you as a woman. I guess I was too wound up in my personal problems."

"Does that mean you're not wound up in them anymore?" she asked softly, slipping her feet out of her shoes and tucking her legs underneath her as if she were settling in for a long talk. Which was not exactly what he had in mind. He didn't want to go in, but he didn't want to stay out here, either. He didn't like talking about his feelings,

past or present, and he wasn't going to start now. But she
was sitting there, looking expectant, waiting...

"Yes, my problems are over now," he admitted. "My
marriage is over, too, and done with. I came out of it with
one thing, the knowledge that it's an institution that's vastly
overrated. Take the mayor and her husband. Did you hear
them bickering over the menu tonight? But don't take my
word for it, Carrie. Try it yourself. That's what you want,
isn't it?" He'd seen how she'd looked in that white dress.
He'd seen the longing in her eyes. Of course she wanted to
get married.

"Not really. I can't say I want to get married. I might
want to marry *somebody,* but marriage in general, no."

He shook his head. If she wanted to marry *somebody,*
that somebody wouldn't have a chance. Not against her
determination. She'd worked hard for what she wanted. To
become a police officer, to get her degree and now this job.
Against all odds. He reached out and ruffled her hair, letting the silky strands sift through his fingers. "Good for
you," he said.

Suddenly it hit him with the force of a hand grenade ex-
ploding overhead. What if she wanted to marry him? What
if this charade became real? He, Matt Graham, who wasn't
afraid of anything, was terrified that Carrie, his partner,
who he'd taught to shoot straight, and who was afraid of
spiders, might want to marry *him.* He withdrew his hand
and got out of the car. He walked around and opened her
door. She didn't move.

"What's wrong?" he asked gruffly.

"I don't have my shoes on," she said in a muffled voice.

"Don't bother." He looked at the gravel path that led to
the house. He couldn't stand there waiting another minute. "I'll carry you," he said. Then he swept her up into his
arms, out of the car and into the foggy night. She wrapped
her arms around his neck. Her cheek fit under his shoulder bone and her scent enveloped him like the fog. He was

tempted to kick the front door open and continue right on up the stairs.

Instead he paused at the doorstep and dumped her on the Welcome mat. He hadn't lost all his sense. Not yet. Adam and Mandy were in front of the fire staring at each other across a card table. They looked up when Matt and Carrie walked in.

"Just in time," Mandy said, "to save our marriage."

"We don't play cards," Carrie said.

"It's Scrabble," Mandy explained. "Just help us finish this one game so we can go to bed. I want Carrie on my side," she said to Adam. "You can have Matt."

Carrie gave Matt a helpless look before she took the chair opposite her hostess. Matt sat across from Adam. He looked at Carrie. She was already arranging her letters. Maybe he was wrong. Maybe she didn't want to marry him after all. Maybe it was wishful thinking on his part.

Suddenly she looked up at him. Mandy looked at him, too, and Adam. It was his turn. He hadn't even looked at his letters. "Sorry," he muttered. He moved the wooden tiles around, staring at them helplessly while the others waited.

Finally he fished out a *t* and *h* and an *e* and put them, in that order, on the board.

Carrie sighed. "Is that the best you can do?" she asked.

"I haven't actually played much Scrabble," he told her with a sideways glare. He'd had no intention of playing any kind of game tonight. He wished he'd refused and gone straight to bed. To bed. The images swam in front of his eyes. Carrie in her pale green negligee with one strap falling over her shoulder, baring her breast. Carrie in that pink teddy. Which would it be tonight? While he daydreamed, the others made words, interesting, challenging words. Carrie spelled out *screak*.

He came back to earth with a thump. "Screak?" he demanded. "Screak?"

She gazed at him calmly. "Challenge me," she urged.

"I'll get the dictionary," Adam offered.

"All right, I challenge you," Matt said. "She's bluffing," he told Adam.

Adam paused. "You sure? She looks pretty confident."

"She always looks that way. It doesn't mean anything."

Carrie raised her eyebrows and smiled smugly. The men stood and conferenced behind her back. Carrie watched Mandy fold her hands over her expanding girth. Then she stood. "I'll make some tea," Mandy said.

Carrie watched her go, wondering if she would ever glow like that, if she would ever have a husband and a baby. Now that she'd had a pretend fiancé, she wanted a real one, then a real husband and a real baby. She fiddled with the letters in front of her, ashamed of herself for feeling envious. Wasn't it enough that she'd gotten a great job, a lovely house and a whole new life? When she'd started on this trip a short time ago, that was all she'd wanted.

Now she wanted it all. And after she had the husband and the baby she would probably want a spa on the patio and then a vacation house at Lake Tahoe. There was no getting around it. She was a selfish, demanding person with no end to her greed.

She'd told Matt she wasn't interested in marriage in general. That much was true. She was only interested in marrying someone special. So special he would have to be handsome, brave, kind, good-humored...well that let Matt out. His good humor was short-lived these days, except when he was planning his coffeehouse.

Part of that was her fault. She kept asking him questions he didn't want to answer. Prying into a past he didn't want uncovered. But he was different. So was she. He'd changed since coming to Moss Beach. Changed for the better. The old Matt would never have played Scrabble or even thought about opening a business. Hardheaded policemen didn't play games or hire rock bands out of high school. They went undercover and arrested drug dealers.

But had he changed enough? Enough to be happy living here? That was wishful thinking. Nobody could change that much that fast. She loved him the way he was. She'd always loved him and she would probably love him forever. He didn't know that and he never would unless she drank too much champagne and lost her inhibitions. Which wasn't going to happen.

Mandy came back with the tea; the men challenged Carrie. They got the dictionary.

"*Screak*," Mandy read out loud. "'To screech or creak.'"

Carrie clenched her fists and raised her arms over her head in victory.

Matt leaned back in his chair and laughed out loud. A warm, rich sound that warmed her heart. They quit after that. Mandy stretched out on the couch and Adam massaged her feet.

"I hate to lose you two," Mandy said with a yawn. "The mayor called to say you'd got your contract and you're moving in tomorrow."

Carrie had hardly heard Mandy when she was discussing the details. Not when Matt was looking at her with his cool gray eyes, and his enigmatic smile. The thought of leaving the bed and breakfast caused her to stop dumping letters into the Scrabble box and look at Matt. How would he feel about moving into her house with her? What if there was only one bed there, too?

They said good-night and went upstairs. Carrie walked to the window and gazed out into the darkness. The last night in this room. The last night to hear the surf below. Matt stayed at the door, as if planning a hasty escape. Finally, he spoke. "There's something I have to tell you."

She braced herself against the window seat, and tried to prepare herself for the worst.

"My intention in coming here was to talk you out of the job," he said.

"I know," she said. "But it didn't work." Nothing anybody did could have talked her out of this job.

"So I tried something else."

She didn't say anything. Here it comes. The confession about the shoes. At least she would get them back.

"I took your shoes."

"No." She turned to look at him.

"Yes." His eyes narrowed. "You knew, didn't you?"

She nodded.

"I don't know what made me think it would make any difference. It was just an impulse. I'll go get them."

"Is that all?" she asked, suddenly relieved.

"No. I left the spider on your desk."

"I didn't know that," she said slowly.

"I'm sorry. It was a bad joke."

She thought of herself in her office, reacting to the rubber spider, making a fool of herself. Matt had done it. Matt, her friend, her partner. She felt a rush of disappointment, the bottom falling out of her world. It was stupid, it was only a joke. She wouldn't cry, so she started to laugh. Anything to break the tension. She wasn't laughing at him, she was laughing at herself. At the memory of herself knocking over the coffee, screaming and running from the room. She must have looked ridiculous. A tear trickled down her cheek. She pressed her lips together and willed herself to stop. This was no time for hysterics. It was time to clear the air.

"That's it?" she asked. She had to know. She had to find out what else he'd done. She couldn't live on daydreams anymore. "What about making me late for work?"

"Yes." He felt miserable. Sick at heart. He wanted to cross the room and take her in his arms, kiss away those tears. But she didn't want that. He could tell by the look in her eyes, the frost in her voice.

"The flat tire?"

"No," he blurted. "I wouldn't do that."

"But the goodbye kiss that morning, the dream the first day... all to make me late?"

He couldn't look at her any longer. "Yes."

"I should have known. I thought you'd changed. That suddenly— But you couldn't... nobody could change that fast. I don't know what I was thinking..." She ran her hands through her red curls and faced the wall. "I thought you'd all of a sudden found me attractive..." she said in a strangled voice.

He clenched his hands into fists. "I found you... *more* than attractive. Everything I did to make you late I *wanted* to do. More than I imagined. More than you know."

She shook her head. "How do you expect me to believe you, after all that?"

"I don't." He exhaled slowly. "All I can say is I'm sorry."

"I am, too," she said with a catch in her voice.

"I'll go get your shoes," he said, and closed the door behind him.

Chapter Nine

Carrie didn't hesitate. Once Matt closed the door behind him, she undressed and put on her granny gown. Furious, she fastened the buttons with shaky fingers. How *could* he have deliberately tried to sabotage her like that? And how could *she* have run screaming from the room at the sight of a *rubber* spider? Lying under the covers, she closed her eyes and tried to suppress the hurt and resentment that threatened to overwhelm her.

She told herself it was flattering to think he'd gone to all that trouble just to get her to come back to L.A. And it was encouraging to hear that he found her attractive. On the other hand, what did it mean? After being seen in a blue uniform and a bulletproof vest day after day, anyone would look attractive in real clothes. He was just reacting to her civilian self, just as she was reacting to the civilian Matt Graham, the guy who took time to walk on the beach, play parlor games and kiss her with unexpected passion. She'd long ago accepted the fact that she was hopelessly in love with her partner. But suddenly, ever since they'd left the smoggy L.A. basin, it hadn't seemed quite so hopeless. Not when she caught him looking at her with a heated gaze, or a reluctant smile, and especially that sideways glance that always set her senses reeling.

She realized now that what she'd felt for him before this trip was admiration, adulation, almost hero worship. Now that she'd seen the not-so-heroic side of Matt Graham, the vulnerable side, that hero worship had turned into something else, something deeper, more complicated. So complicated, she didn't understand it very well. She only knew they only had a few more days together. A few more days and a few more nights. Thank heavens.

Matt was back in the room before she'd had a chance to sort out her thoughts any further. "Get dressed," he said. "There's been another typical Moss Beach crime."

She slid out of bed and grabbed a pair of pants. "What, another drunk at the campground?"

He shook his head. "Stolen horse at the riding stable."

She pulled her pants on under her nightgown with her back to him. "I don't know how to find a stolen horse in broad daylight, let alone in the dark," she protested.

He turned his back to her while she tossed on a shirt, then socks and shoes. "Look for clues," he advised. "Ask questions. You know how. You've been in burglary."

"Yes, but whenever you and I solved a burglary, it was because somebody dropped a dime on the perp," she said as they tiptoed down the stairs so as not to wake the other guests.

"So maybe we've got a witness who'll drop a dime and come forward," he suggested.

We. Carrie realized as they drove down the quiet streets that there was no "we" anymore. She alone was responsible for solving crimes in Moss Beach. Granted, they didn't seem very serious, but nonetheless, the town expected her to solve them. Without Matt to back her up, to be a sounding board, to bounce ideas off. To share a late-night coffee after writing a report. "We couldn't have done it without our informants," she mused. How long would it take to build up a group of informants like the ones she'd left behind?

They pulled up in front of the ramshackle stables with the Coastside Equestrian Center sign tilted to one side over the gate. The owner, a florid-faced, overweight man in his mid-fifties, greeted them at the gate and gave them the details.

Business had been slow, the horses had been in the pasture during the day. When he'd gone to bring them in tonight, one was missing—a bay mare with a white star.

After writing this down in her notebook, Carrie looked at the man. "Could she possibly be a runaway?"

"Why would she run away?" the owner asked irritably. "She's got everything she wants right here. Food and lodging. And not much to do."

"Could we see the stable?"

The man shrugged and led them to the empty stall. The smell was overwhelming. "How often do you clean the stalls?" Carrie asked with a frown.

"Whenever I can get someone to work for me, but the high school kids around here don't want to work. Probably one of them who stole her. I would have gone looking myself, but I heard we got a police chief, why not let him do it? Didn't know you'd be a woman," he said, disgruntled.

Carrie knew it wouldn't be the last time she'd hear that, so she kept her mouth closed. And when Matt opened his mouth to protest, she nudged him in the ribs. She and Matt walked the perimeter of the pasture. With her flashlight they looked for a break in the fence, then went back to the stable and she told the owner she would keep him informed.

"What next?" Matt asked as they walked back to the car.

"Doesn't it remind you of that missing person report we got on a teenager about a year ago? Same thing, the parents couldn't understand why she'd leave, she had everything."

"Turned out she was mistreated and ran away. I see the connection, yes. But there we went around and asked her friends, went to her school."

They sat in the car, and Carrie stared straight ahead into the darkness. She hadn't spent so much time in a car with Matt since they'd been on surveillance a year ago. She'd miss the long, comfortable silences, the shared confidences, the whispered conferences. "Yeah," she said. "I'll bet those horses in there could tell us what happened. They could set us straight in about five minutes. Unfortunately I don't understand them."

"I can't help you there," he said. "I don't even understand people." He turned to face her. The pale moon cast a shadow across his face. "You, for example. I thought we had a good thing going in L.A. And you throw it all away for this. Chasing horses around in the middle of the night. Is this really what you want?"

"Of course it isn't," she admitted. "But how often will I be called out for a runaway horse?"

"That's right. Next time it might be a pet parakeet who's flown the coop."

Carrie pressed her lips together to keep from retorting. She was tired of arguing with him. Tired of standing up for her new way of life, for the town and the people in it. Matt would never give in and neither would she. And the fact was, he was wearing her down. Making her wonder if once the novelty wore off she might get bored.

She might even be lonely without him. She wondered what she would do if he flat-out asked her to come back with him. If he told her it was more than breaking in a new partner. If he said he would miss her. That he cared about her. He didn't love her. She knew that. He would never love again. But maybe she didn't need to be loved. She would rather love than be loved. That's what counted.

She rested her head on the headrest. It might happen anytime, any place. At her new house, in the living room for example, with a fire blazing in her own fireplace. The first fire of the season. A sheepskin rug on the hearth. He would be packed and ready to go. But he couldn't go. Not without her. He needed her, wanted her, and told her so. At last. She would pack her suitcase and walk out the door with him and live happily ever after. Where, in L.A.?

What about her job, the town and her house? Could she give all that up for Matt? She snuck a glance at his profile, the determined set of his jaw, his dark hair falling over his forehead. Forget it. It wasn't going to happen. He wasn't going to ask her. Not now. Not ever.

They drove around the rural area, up and down winding country roads, looking for the horse, shining their flashlight into empty corrals, but they didn't see any bay mare with a star on her forehead.

They finally went back to the inn and went to bed. Carrie wore her flannel nightgown. She didn't know what he wore. She closed her eyes and tried to forget about Matt's treachery, Matt's leaving and the runaway horse.

Carrie felt better in the morning, especially after she'd checked in at the office, then walked to her house when she heard the movers had arrived. The mayor had chosen the furniture; the city council okayed the purchase. Carrie stood in the front yard watching the movers struggle with a king-size bed, and her heart sputtered. Another big bed to share. So big, the movers had to take it apart to get it up the stairs.

"Got your stove and fridge," the moving-van driver told her. "You can eat in tonight." Great, just what she wanted. A cozy dinner for two in her new dining room. So that ever after as she sat alone looking across the green fields from the dining room she would think of Matt and feel lonely. She would remember him sitting across the table from her, feel a lump in her throat, and go back to the kitchen.

That morning Carrie had called the county animal control and the humane society, who promised to investigate the conditions at the stables. Then she posted flyers around town with a description of the missing horse.

Next she was scheduled to give a talk at the high school about drugs and alcohol. Hopefully the kids here were a little more innocent than those she'd spoken to before— kids who could have taught her more than she'd ever taught them.

As she spoke she imagined her own kids attending the sprawling high school surrounded by green soccer fields, only a short distance from the beach. She would come to open house, join the PTA, help them with their homework, comb their hair in the mornings... No, not if they were in high school. She shook herself out of her reverie and passed out bumper stickers and posters urging kids to say no to alcohol and drugs.

When she got back to the office she found a message from an abalone fisherman who'd had his nets pilfered and lost a sizable investment in abalone he'd been farming along the coast. She called to tell him she would be out to investigate as soon as she could. But she had no more idea how to track down stolen abalone than a stolen horse. Wait till Matt heard about this.

She suddenly longed for the good old days when she and Matt were assigned to one thing—burglary, robbery or homicide. Now all of a sudden she was a one-woman department, specializing, it seemed, in missing animals.

At five o'clock she walked home from work. She loved the idea of it. She loved the fact that she could be home in ten minutes. So much for commuting in frantic freeway traffic leaving her nerves shot. Tonight her nerves were frazzled for entirely different reasons. Matt leaving, lost animals, the need to prove herself to the town.

She passed Matt's coffeehouse and saw him in the middle of the room setting up chairs with a group of high school kids. His face was creased with dirt, his forehead lined with worry.

"Tonight's your opening," she said. "Are you nervous?"

"Me nervous about opening a coffeehouse?" He nodded ruefully. "I guess I am. I don't know why I'm doing this. No one's going to come."

"Are you kidding?" she said. "Everyone's coming. Everyone I've talked to." She put her hand on his shoulder to reassure him, feeling the muscles under the soft, worn cotton of his sweatshirt. "Are you coming home for dinner?"

He stared at her for a moment. Home. She shouldn't have said it. It just slipped out. It wasn't his home. It wasn't *their* home.

"I'll be too busy," he said.

She withdrew her hand and went home by herself. So much for her vision of their dinner together in the dining room. She ate by herself in the kitchen. Get used to it, she told herself. Get used to solving crimes by yourself, eating and sleeping by yourself, too. Because you made your choice. You chose one place over another. Forgetting about the people, the person, she hadn't really known until now all that she'd be giving up. But now that she did know, there was nothing she could do about it. She gave up trying to eat and put her plate into her new dishwasher.

She wandered over to the coffeehouse about eight-thirty, hoping it would be a big success for Matt's sake. To make him see he could succeed at something other than police work. The crowd was lined up around the block. There were loud high school boys with long hair and earrings, long-legged girls in tight jeans along with a middle-aged crowd. Carrie waved to the manager of the sewage plant and the high school principal. Adam came up to talk to her.

"This is the greatest thing since the railroad arrived in 1887. I was just telling Matt I hope he stays around longer than the trains did."

Carrie wondered how Matt had felt when he'd heard that. Wondered how he'd felt when he'd seen the people lined up around the block. She didn't catch a glimpse of him all evening. She didn't even get near the coffeehouse. It was too crowded. She sat on the curb next to the mayor while Her Honor enthused over the success of Matt's idea.

After a few hours, the music tapered off, the crowd dispersed and Carrie got up and stretched, feeling numb from the loud music and her position on the curb. She pressed her nose against the plate-glass window and looked at the old bar covered with paper cups and crumpled napkins.

Matt came in from the back room, looked at the outline of her body in the light of the streetlight and went to the window. He spread his hands flat against the glass on either side of her face. He thought she would have left by now. He wasn't even sure she'd come. She looked as tired as he felt, but she smiled at him and he felt a weight lift from his shoulders. Maybe she didn't hate him after all, even after all he'd done.

Now if he could only keep his cool until he left town, he could leave feeling he'd done his best and have no regrets. He turned out the lights, went outside and locked the door behind him. "How'd you like it?" he asked, keeping his arms at his sides. If he didn't he would slide one arm around her waist, pull her to him, feel her hip against his as they walked home. But he didn't have a home. Never had, never would.

"It was great. Everyone said so. How do you feel?" She looked up into his eyes and he felt himself weakening. What harm would it do to have one last night together? Really together. He knew the answer. If he had one, he would want another and another, and he would never leave. He would be stuck in this place for the rest of his productive life.

"I thought it worked out pretty well. There are things I'd do next time, if there was a next time."

"But there won't be." They walked slowly up the street to her house.

"Not unless someone else takes it over." He didn't know how he would feel about that, somebody else using the machines he'd rented. Grinding the beans he'd bought. It was *his* coffeehouse, *his* idea.

They paused for a moment in front of her house. The porch light she'd left on cast a welcoming glow through the darkness. "I envy you," he said before he could stop himself.

She didn't ask why. She seemed to know. It was true. He envied anyone who had everything they wanted—the job, the town and the house. She walked up to the front door and opened it. "Want something to eat?" she asked over her shoulder flicking on the lamp on the living room table.

He stared. The room was full of furniture. Strange furniture. Probably purchased for her by the town and chosen by somebody else. But suddenly it looked like Carrie. Large, comfortable chairs, polished tables, even a fireplace with a fire laid. Hardwood floors with a sheepskin rug on the hearth.

"Sounds good," he said. When she went into the kitchen, he bent over and lit the fire. It was after midnight. He was exhausted. Physically and mentally. She must be, too. But he couldn't go to bed yet. He had things to say. And he wasn't looking forward to saying them.

He slumped into an easy chair and watched, hypnotized, as the flames sputtered and crackled and came to life. When Carrie came back into the room with a bowl of hot soup in her hands, he met her gaze and didn't look away. She knows, he thought. She knows what's coming. And after all, she would probably be glad to have him gone. To be rid of his constant ragging on the town. Just as he would be glad to get back to the real world. She set the soup on the coffee table, then sat down on the fur rug, crossed her legs underneath her and looked into the dancing flames.

"I thought I'd take off tomorrow," he said abruptly, ignoring the lump in his throat the size of a cannonball.

She nodded. She didn't even look at him. She wasn't surprised. How could she be? She expected it. "I have to thank you," she said, keeping her eyes on the fire.

"Carrie," he blurted. "Don't thank me. I feel terrible about this." There was a pain in his chest that got worse every time she spoke. Why did she have to be so damned understanding?

"Why should you feel terrible?" she asked, turning halfway toward him. "You've done me a huge favor. One I can never repay. If I can, I hope you'll let me know. Look around you. Everything I have here is because of you."

"What if they take it all away when I leave?" he asked, gripping his soupspoon in his hand.

She shook her head. "They won't. They can't. I read the small print in the contract. What they asked was illegal anyway. They can't use marital status as a requirement for a civil job. You know that. I overlooked it because I wanted it so much. And I understand, I really do. They want me to stay here forever. And I'm going to." She shifted, letting her chin drop onto her knees. "This is a family kind of place. People grow up here and raise their children here. I don't blame them for wanting me to do the same."

He studied the back of her head, her red hair tumbling over her shoulders, and he felt his chest tighten. She wouldn't do it, would she? Raise children here?

"I just hope they don't blame me," she continued.

"They won't," he assured her. "Not when you tell them what happened." He stirred his soup so vigorously he was afraid the bowl might crack. "That I walked out on you."

"I guess not," she said. "After all, what could I do to stop you? Throw myself in front of your car?"

He tried to smile but his mouth wouldn't cooperate. "That's not your style," he said. He thought for a moment. "I don't suppose . . . no."

"What?" she asked, tilting her head in his direction.

There was a long silence. She was waiting, but he couldn't say it. Couldn't ask her to come back with him. Not now. it was too late. And he knew what she would say. Frustration pumped through his veins. "Nothing," he finally said and forced himself to sip his soup.

"So you were pleased with your coffeehouse," she said in an obvious attempt at changing the subject. "Whatever gave you the idea?"

"I used to hang out at this coffeehouse in Anaheim," he said, leaning back against the cushions of the big chair. "The owner was a guy I once busted for illegal possession who went straight and opened a café. He invited me over, would never let me pay and talked my ear off. He knew I appreciated a good bean. Taught me the difference between arabica and robusta. I envied him, sitting around talking to customers all day. So relaxed. I thought if I ever retired, I'd do something like that. It's a fantasy, of course. I'm not going to retire."

"Even when you're sixty-five?" she asked, looking up at him with a half smile on her face.

"Maybe then."

"Maybe you'll come back up here," she suggested lightly.

Matt pictured himself hobbling into town, his body bruised and beaten from years of abuse on the beat, his hair gray, his chin grizzled, to find Carrie surrounded by her grandchildren, her husband, the well digger, and the townsfolk who hadn't forgotten he'd deserted her, left her standing at the altar as it were, at the historic Delarosa House wearing that white dress with the miracle bra and the cinched waist... He closed his eyes as a spasm of pain ripped through his gut.

"What's wrong?" she asked.

"Just wondering what they'll do with those wedding clothes."

"Return them, I guess."

"Unless you find someone else to take my place," he suggested. He didn't understand why he was torturing himself this way. Why he didn't just talk about coffee some more?

She shook her head. "I'll be too busy solving crimes to do any man-hunting."

"Don't let them work you too hard." But that's just what he wanted. For her to work too hard to look for a husband. Because when Carrie wanted something she usually got it. Which made him realize she didn't really want him or she would say something. Do something. But she'd done nothing but be understanding and grateful. He didn't even know if she was still awake. Her eyes were closed, her head tilted back, her hair gleaming red-gold in the firelight. She should go to bed. So should he. But where?

He still had things to say before he left. He just didn't know how to say them. He'd never been good at goodbyes. He never wanted to let anyone know how he felt down deep. So he often didn't know himself. Hell, most of the time he didn't want to feel. It was too painful.

"I hope...you'll be okay when I leave," he began.

"Of course I will. I don't want to play the jilted bride role, any more than you want to be the bad guy. Maybe I'll just tell the truth for a change. Oh, not the whole truth," she assured him. "That the whole thing was a sham. And we were never engaged. I mean the truth about why you're leaving."

He stared at her. Why *was* he leaving? Maybe she had the answer. Because right now with the firelight making her face glow like a gem, her brown eyes as soft as velvet, he wanted to reach over and pull her into his lap. To make love right there on the rug with the flames making shadows on their bodies.

He wanted to ask her to ask him to stay. But he couldn't do that. She would say no. She had her own life to lead and she didn't need him anymore. She'd gotten this job on her own, no matter what she thought. His part was over. No matter how natural it seemed to come home to this house and to her, it wasn't natural at all. What was natural was to return to the station, to the streets, the courts, the challenges.

"The truth," he repeated. "Sure, tell them the truth."

"I'll say you missed L.A. That small-town life just didn't agree with you. Is that okay?" She rested her head against his knees and he felt a shudder go through his body. He nodded. Of course it was okay. But was it true? He couldn't speak.

"I'll miss you, Matt," she said with a catch in her voice. God, what was wrong with her? She'd promised herself she wouldn't cry. She wouldn't get sentimental. But if she didn't say it now she might never have another chance. Why didn't he reach down and take her by the shoulders? What more did she have to do? She ought to be happy he was so restrained. Instead she felt frustrated and disappointed. Couldn't he even say he would miss her, too?

"Carrie." His voice was taut with tension, but she didn't turn around. "This hasn't turned out the way I thought it would. I thought you were crazy to want to come up here, but now I understand."

She didn't want him to understand her. She wanted him to want her, to love her and never leave her. She thought he might ask her again to go back with him. If he did, she would go. She knew in a sudden flash that whatever she had here, she would give it up to follow him back there. Call it love, call it insanity, she just knew she would do it. Because they were partners. In every sense of the word,

Without him she would never be whole. Without him she would never be complete. Why hadn't she realized it before? Before it was too late?

"It's late," she said in a bare whisper, pulling herself to her feet.

"I'll sleep down here. That way I won't wake you when I leave in the morning." There, he'd said it. He was leaving in the morning. He stood and stretched, and carefully avoided her eyes.

"I'll get you a blanket." Her feet felt like lead as she climbed the stairs to the linen closet. He didn't want to sleep with her, not even next to her. Not anymore. It wasn't necessary. She had the job. There was no one around to fool. Her tears were so close to the surface she bit her lip to hold them back.

When she came back with the blanket in her arms he was standing at the window looking out into the still, dark night. "I never thought I'd get used to the silence around here," he said without turning around. "There's nobody out there, nothing happening."

"I *hope* there's nothing happening. I hope there won't be an emergency every night."

"If there is," he said, turning to face her, "don't go by yourself. Take somebody along. Appoint a deputy. Do you hear me?" he demanded.

"I hear you but, Matt, this is Moss Beach." She sighed. "Oh, all right." She dropped the blanket on the couch. "But what about you? You're in more danger than I am. What about that guy who's out to get you? Have they caught him yet? If I were there . . ." She would be there to back him up, to insist on his being careful.

"You'd just be in the way," he said. "I'll have a new partner."

He didn't have to remind her. She felt bad enough thinking of someone else sharing his office, his patrol car, his life. . . .

"Some idiot right out of the academy probably. Full of theories and no experience," he continued.

"Isn't that what you thought of me?"

"You had some sense, at least." He lifted her chin with his knuckles and scanned her face. "And a lot of freckles."

She felt the corners of her mouth turn up even as she fought back the tears his tenderness provoked. "I always thought freckles were a disadvantage."

"So did I," he said under his breath, "until now." Gently he kissed each freckle on her face. Then the tension that had been building all evening snapped. He cupped her head with his hand and opened his mouth to devour her as if there was no tomorrow. And for them there wasn't.

She gave in to his kiss without a second thought, knowing it was for the last time. Mindlessly her hands moved to his face, her fingers tracing the rough outline of his jaw, while he pulled her tight against him. Their kisses got frantic, wild, making up for the way they'd held back for so long. He backed her up to the couch. She sank into the cushions and pulled him down on top of her.

She loved the weight of him, the steel of his muscles pressing down on her, filling every hollow and crevice with his manhood. She wound her arms around his neck, let her fingers sift through his thick dark hair, inhaling the smell of him, of fresh air and coffee.

His kisses drifted down her throat. Propping himself on one elbow, he lifted the edge of her shirt. He cupped her breasts in his hands. His gaze was full of questions, but he knew the answer. Yes, yes, yes. His warm breath, then his mouth on the sensitive tips of her breasts caused her exquisite agony.

"Matt," she begged.

He misunderstood. With a supreme effort, he raised himself up and took a deep breath. "I'm sorry. I don't know what happened."

"Nothing happened," she protested. But she wanted it to. Needed it, craved it.

"It won't," he promised, pulling her shirt back in place with one unsteady hand. "It can't happen. There's no future in it."

"There doesn't have to be." What did she have to do, spell it out?

"You'd be sorry tomorrow," he said, his voice dropping low.

"I'd rather be sorry tomorrow than tonight," she blurted. "I wish we'd never come here."

He pulled her up by the shoulders to face him. Pain and regret and sorrow lurked in the depths of his gray eyes. "You don't mean that."

She pulled away from him. "I do mean it. I'm sorry we came. I'm sorry you're leaving, and I'm sorry I fell apart like this." She gulped, hanging on to her pride by a narrow thread. She'd almost said it, told him how she felt. But she'd stopped just in time. He would never know how she felt about him. Not if he didn't know now.

He tucked a strand of hair behind her ear, so gently it made her heart ache. "Good luck," he said, standing unsteadily. "If there's ever anything I can do..."

She shook her head and got up from the couch. He'd done enough already. Way too much. She turned and ran up the stairs before she lost what little dignity she had left and begged him to take her back with him.

Chapter Ten

Matt was up at dawn after a sleepless night. He'd lain on the couch. He'd sat on the couch with his head buried in his hands. Then he'd paced back and forth in front of the couch, replaying the last goodbye over and over in his mind, and thinking he'd almost made love to her on that couch.

She wanted it. He wanted it. But he'd come to his senses just in time. If they'd given in to their passion he wouldn't be driving mindlessly down the freeway while the mist rose from the fields on either side of the road and the sun hovered on the horizon and glared in his eyes. No, he would be back in bed with her, in her new house, in the room overlooking the garden with the smell of roses wafting in the window.

He wouldn't have left. He would have made breakfast for her and brought it to her bed. He would have walked her to work. Waited for her to come home at night. He shuddered. A house husband. He would never be able to leave her, and his life would dribble away in that one-horse town

One horse. His eyes swept the landscape for a bay mare with a star on her forehead. As if she could have gotten this far. Where was she, then? Would Carrie ever find her? It wasn't his problem, he knew, but her problems had always been his problems. Force of habit. They'd been partners so long. Too long. It was time for her to branch out on her own. Take control. He would worry about her, but the truth was she had everything it took—skill, nerves and intelligence—to succeed on her own, and she didn't need him anymore.

It hurt to admit it. He rubbed his eyes to keep them from closing. He'd forgotten how boring this ride was, how repetitious the scenery. On the way up, the time had flown by. They'd talked, stopped for lunch. Matt didn't want to stop. He wanted to drive straight through. Get home before dark. Home? He didn't have a home. Not even an apartment to call home.

He would check into a motel near the station, look for an efficiency tomorrow. He looked at his watch. Carrie would be up now, having breakfast at the round oak table in her new kitchen with the pine cupboards, before she walked to work. On her way she would pass the coffeehouse. He should have told her to put a sign in the window—Closed Until Further Notice. She would probably do it anyway. She thought of everything. But did she think about him? Probably not.

All the way back he fought off fatigue, drowsiness and depression. Matt tried to think ahead and not dwell on the past. But it was a losing battle. Every hour, every minute of that interminable drive he thought about where she was and what she was doing.

He'd done the right thing by not making love to her. But the memory of her soft lips, the smooth satin of her skin and her dark, luminous eyes looking reproachful haunted him. Thinking of the opportunities lost, he gripped the steering wheel so hard his knuckles turned white. He turned on the radio to drown out his thoughts with loud country music until he pulled off the freeway at last and found a nondescript motel in his old neighborhood. He told himself things would be back to normal soon. But he couldn't remember what normal was anymore.

Carrie had curled up in a chair by her bedroom window with a quilt tucked around her and stayed there all night. She'd waited for dawn, listening for Matt's car to start, forcing herself to stay where she was instead of running downstairs and begging him to stay. There was nothing she could say that would make him change his mind. She'd just sat there, picturing him driving down the street, back the way they'd come.

After he'd left she'd roused herself, gotten dressed and gone downstairs. Her footsteps echoed down the hall. *You're alone, alone, alone,* said a voice inside her head. She put a jacket over her dress and went to work. Yes, it was an hour early, but she had things to do. The first was to forget about Matt. To stop wondering where he would stop, to stop feeling like a fool for begging him to make love to her.

She knew he didn't love her. But she hoped he would remember her sometimes with fondness, with respect for the way she was before she'd come unglued these past weeks. Hopefully he would remember her as his levelheaded partner, the one in the blue uniform and not the pink silk teddy.

Carrie passed the coffeehouse on the way to work. There was no other way to get there. Only a smashed paper cup on the sidewalk gave an indication of what went on the night before. Carrie picked up the cup and crumpled it in her hand. The fog blew in off the ocean and crept around the corner of Main Street. Carrie shivered inside her jacket and pulled the collar up around her chin.

Soon she was going to have to tell people. But even now, she still didn't know what to say. She didn't want to sound pathetic. But she didn't want to sound callous, either, as if she didn't care. How to strike the right balance, that was the problem. Especially when she was feeling so very much off balance right now.

If she got to work before anyone else, she would have time to practice her speech. "It just didn't work out," she murmured to herself as she let herself into her office. "It wasn't anybody's fault." Nobody's fault? It was her fault. Her fault for asking Matt to come with her. But did she ask or did he volunteer? Everything that had happened before they'd come to Moss Beach was a blur.

People could say what they wanted about nothing happening in small towns, but these past days had been packed so full they became a kaleidoscope of images in her mind. She and Matt at the potluck. Matt applauding the speech she'd given to the Elks club. Matt taking her shoes at the beach. Waking up wrapped in Matt's arms at the B and B, feeling so warm, so happy, so *right*. As if all her dreams had suddenly come true.

She sat at her desk with her hands wrapped around a cup of hot coffee she'd brewed in the kitchen. She thought of how Matt would take a sip and shake his head in disgust. "Too acidic," he would say, or "Too bitter." There was a knock on her door and Carrie almost spilled another cup all over her desk. She jumped to her feet and let the mayor in. It was here—the moment she'd dreaded since she'd first dreamed up this scheme.

"I saw your light on," Mayor Thompson said, taking the chair opposite Carrie's desk. "May I?" Carrie nodded. "You're here early."

"Yes," she said. Say it, she told herself. Tell her why you're in early today. Why you look like something the cat dragged in. Why you didn't sleep last night, and why you couldn't eat breakfast this morning. She'll understand. She might understand too well. Understand how Carrie had lied about having a fiancé, had tricked the town into hiring her. Unless she showed some emotion about what happened.

The emotion part wasn't hard. As soon as Carrie opened her mouth and explained that Matt had broken their engagement, the tears came fast and furiously. The tears she'd been holding back. The pain came, too, the pain that gripped her heart and squeezed like a vise. The mayor looked startled, but quickly produced a handful of tissues and a warm pat on the back.

"He'll be back," Maggie told Carrie.

Carrie walked to the window, her back to the mayor, and shook her head, unable to speak, to tell her she was wrong.

"Then you'll find someone else," the older woman assured her.

Carrie nodded. Sure she would. Someone else to replace the man she'd been in love with the past two years? Not likely.

"You're upset and hurt. I understand. But you'll get over it. When you're my age you'll realize that no man is worth crying over. Though I must admit your Matt was quite a guy—" She broke off. "Oh, I'm sorry."

Carrie managed to give the mayor a watery smile. "That's all right. If you could just explain to the rest of the city council."

"Of course," the mayor assured her with a sympathetic smile. "You just take some time off if you need to."

"No," she blurted. "I have to... I want to keep busy. In fact I've got some stolen abalone to track down, as well as a missing horse."

The mayor nodded and Carrie went out and got into the official police car, an unmarked compact sedan. Which reminded her of her own car sitting in Matt's garage. She missed her car, but she missed Matt more. She'd been preparing for this moment for two weeks, and now that it was here, she ought to be able to handle the emptiness, the futility of her life. She'd expected a let-down, but not this... this hollow feeling in the pit of her stomach.

As she snapped photographs of the scene of the crime at the fish hatchery, she told herself things would get better. She stared at the beautiful iridescent abalone shells, but her deductive powers seemed to have deserted her. Now when she needed them. She had no clue, literally, how to track down the delectable and expensive shellfish. If Matt were here...

But he wasn't. She was on her own now.

Fortunately there were no more crimes against either animals or people for several weeks. That gave Carrie plenty of time to try to solve the two already in front of her. She'd told Matt she was tired of crime and violence. But now she was faced with the problem of being a police chief in a town where there was no crime. And if there was, it appeared she couldn't solve it.

The mayor didn't seem worried about it. She was only worried about finding Carrie a replacement for Matt. Carrie remembered thinking about finding a "normal" man once she'd left L.A., and sure enough, thanks to Mayor Maggie, in the space of several weeks, Carrie had met every normal man within a fifty-mile radius. And they *were* normal, so normal Carrie wondered if she wasn't. Normal, that is. Because they weren't interesting. She was willing to give up on finding a man, but the town wasn't. They were all determined to find her someone.

"You know, Carrie," Maggie said one evening as Carrie was about to leave the office, "I'm not concerned about your commitment to the town. That has nothing to do with my interest in introducing you to eligible men. I'm concerned about you." The mayor's forehead wrinkled into a worried frown.

Carrie knew where this was leading, to another blind date with someone Maggie had dug up for her. Some upstanding citizen like the town dentist or a highway worker just dying to go out with the police chief. Not. Men were scared of her. She suspected the mayor had had to do some serious arm-twisting to coerce them into taking her out.

"You've been so understanding," she told the older woman. "I just need some time to get over..." A tear rolled down her cheek. It wasn't planned, but maybe now Maggie would see Carrie was not emotionally fit to start a new relationship. Maybe she would leave her alone for a few years while she recovered.

At this rate it might take ten or twenty years. She thought she'd be better by now. But she was getting worse. "Sorry," Carrie sniffed. "I don't know what's wrong with me."

Maggie walked Carrie to the door. "What do you hear from... I mean, are you—" Her Honor broke off in mid-sentence.

"I haven't heard from Matt," Carrie told her. "I don't expect to." Just because she jumped every time the phone rang and hurried home at noon to check her mailbox didn't mean she expected to hear from Matt. She had nothing to say to him and vice versa.

But as the weeks dragged by she thought about him more, not less. And she began to wonder whether she'd made a big mistake coming to Moss Beach. Was half of Matt's life, the half he shared with her at work, worth more than none at all? While she was pondering, the horse with the white star on its forehead turned itself in. Carrie did the only thing she could. She put the animal in protective custody with a loving family until the stables were cleaned up to her satisfaction. The owner was angry about it, but Carrie didn't back down.

That left the abalone. But a police chief could spend only so much time searching for fish that had most certainly been eaten by now. She would have to say that she wasn't tense after a day at work. Not like she used to be. She wasn't tense, she was... bored. Matt was right. It was her own fault. There were things to do, the weekly flower market, the garden club, the hiking group. She just couldn't bring herself to become involved with them.

In time even the stolen abalone mystery was solved. She didn't take credit. She gave it to the department of fish and game who'd arrested the thieves when they'd come back for a second helping at the fish farm. She admitted it was the most exciting thing that had happened to her since Matt left, which wasn't saying much. It involved laying a trap for the poachers at the hatchery, which the criminals fell right into. Literally.

Fish and Game had made the arrest, but the local newspaper did a story that made her out to be the heroine, describing how she'd been hit on the head with a fishing rod in the fracas. Carrie knew she'd never been in real danger; she'd been unconscious for only a moment, and when she'd come to, the fish and game warden had had it all wrapped up.

But if the town wanted to treat her like their savior, well, why not? It wasn't as good as being a bride in a historic landmark, but she was doing her best to please them. She didn't want to ever see that house on the outskirts of town ever again, and so far she hadn't been by once. It would have hurt to remember the day she'd posed in the white dress, how she'd stood there looking at Matt. And as long as she didn't have to see the house, she wouldn't think about how she wouldn't be getting married there.

"Hey, look at this." Buck Quin burst into Matt's office, the one he'd shared with Carrie once upon a time, and thrust a newspaper in front of Matt's eyes.

Matt glanced at the heading—former L.A. Cop Catches Abalone Poachers. He grabbed the paper out of Buck's hands.

"That's her. That's your Carrie," Buck said. "Did you know about this? What's she doing up there anyway?"

"Just what it says," Matt snapped. "Enforcing law and order... 'Slightly injured,' it says. What the hell does that mean?" he demanded, running his hand through his hair. "I'd better call her." He looked up the number and picked up the phone without thinking. Without remembering he'd promised himself he wouldn't have any contact with her. Without thinking that getting in touch with her was just postponing his recovery. The recovery that he'd been striving for, waiting for, but that hadn't come.

He still thought about her all day, every day. He worried about her being on her own, and now look what had happened. She'd probably gone out there without her gun. He could just hear her say, "But Matt, this is Moss Beach." She didn't listen to him. She thought she knew best. She didn't answer her phone. He was about to slam down the receiver when the mayor answered.

"Lieutenant Graham," the mayor aid, her voice tinged with surprise and pleasure. "Carrie's not here. She's taking the day off. I insisted. It's just a bump on the head, the doctor says, but I thought—"

"A bump on the head?" He gripped the receiver tightly in his hand. "That's all, are you sure?" He was beginning to feel ridiculous for overreacting, but it could be a concussion.

"She's fine. She's a heroine around here. Naturally the town was disappointed when you... when you didn't..."

"Yes, I know. I'm sorry about that," Matt said curtly. He didn't want to hear how sorry everyone was. Nobody was sorrier than he was.

"You can reach her at home," the mayor prompted.

"No... no, now that I know she's okay, that's really all that I...that she... I mean..." What was wrong with him? He couldn't seem to finish a sentence. He was incoherent with relief. He wasn't going to call her at home. Was he crazy? Especially with Buck standing there in his office, watching him, listening. He said goodbye and hung up.

"Well," he said to Buck. "That's it, she's fine. As usual, they exaggerate these things in the press."

"Quite a woman, that Carrie," Buck mused. "D'you ever miss her?"

"Miss her? No." Only when he got to work in the morning and went out on patrol or when he had a problem and no one to talk it over with. Or when he saw his new partner sitting across the room at Carrie's desk.

There were also times when he went to lunch alone or on a coffee break. But worst of all was when he lay in bed at night in his new apartment, which was a lot like his old apartment, trying to sleep, trying not to think about Carrie in that huge feather bed, with her hair spread out on the pillow in a glorious red splash. He reached out as if to touch her, but she wasn't there. No, he didn't miss her. Not at all.

While he lay in bed at night he also thought about the parolee who was out to get him. He heard imaginary noises in his kitchen and went in with his gun cocked. This continued until the guy was picked up for running a red light and was now back behind bars. So Matt could rest easy. But he didn't.

He was still thinking about Carrie suffering a possible concussion, wrestling with the idea of phoning her again, when he was called out on domestic violence. A woman answered the door, for him and his partner, on one of the streets behind Grauman's Chinese Theatre. A short, overweight blonde with a black eye turning purple, she'd phoned in the complaint.

"What's the problem?" Matt asked, looking over her shoulder.

"My husband beat me up," she said, twisting her hands together.

Matt looked her over. Besides the eye, he saw bruises on her jaw and forehead. "What do you want me to do with him?" he asked.

"Take him away," she said.

Matt edged past the woman and his partner and found her husband slouched in front of a giant TV as if nothing had happened. He snapped a pair of cuffs on the man, read him his rights and took him downstairs. He couldn't believe how easy this was going to be. The wife followed them down the stairs, muttering to herself.

As Matt went through the doorway he felt a sudden jolt and a shaft of pain as the woman slammed a butcher knife between his shoulder blades. He remembered thinking he should have worn his vest. He remembered thinking that nothing was so unpredictable as domestic violence, but he didn't remember his partner subduing the wife or calling the medics.

After he came out of surgery they told him what had happened. The woman had been upset with her husband for beating her up until she'd seen him being hauled off by the big, bad policeman. It was just human nature; he knew that even through the fog of the anesthesia. The police are always the villains.

They told him he was lucky she'd missed his spinal cord. He didn't feel lucky. He felt terrible. Stupid and careless and terrible. He lay there for what seemed like weeks but was really only days with what they called a severe subcutaneous infection from the wound. People from work came to see him. But he didn't have the energy to talk. The doctors had him loaded down with painkillers and antibiotics. Buck Quin asked if he should call Carrie.

Matt shook his head. He felt tears sting the backs of his eyelids, thinking he hadn't called her when she was hurt. He didn't want her to know he was lying in a hospital bed while the medics experimented with different medicines, trying to find one that worked. He didn't want her to know how careless he'd been. First neglecting to wear his vest, then ignoring the woman with the knife.

He drifted off into a restless sleep, not knowing when Buck left. Only knowing he was alone, more alone than

he'd ever been in his life. And cold, so cold he thought he
would never be warm again.

When he came to, his head was on fire. He was burning
up. He tried to throw off the sheet, but he didn't have the
strength. He felt a cool smooth hand on his forehead, then
a cup of crushed ice at his lips to quench his burning thirst.
He squinted at a blaze of copper-colored hair and dark eyes
gazing into his. He tried to swallow, but there was a lump
in his throat. He was delirious.

He thought he saw Carrie on the edge of his bed, hov-
ering on the periphery of his vision. He even thought it was
her hand on his brow. As if she weren't six hundred miles
away solving crimes of her own, with more success than
he'd had. To think he'd worried about her. He almost
laughed. If only he could make his mouth move. Ask who
she was, this angel of mercy.

"Matt." She took his hands in hers, that cool smooth
hand that he'd held before. In another life. Before he got
sick. Before he left Carrie. She pressed his hand against her
cheek, and he felt her tears. He wanted to tell her not to cry.
He was okay. But all he could do was squeeze her hand. He
couldn't even open his eyes. He drifted away.

The next thing he knew the doctor said they were going
to try something else. It had a long name. The woman
asked a question. She sounded worried. The doctor told her
he was doing everything he could. He talked about swollen
lymph glands, intravenous antibiotics. Then the room got
quiet. In the hall someone was being paged. Somewhere
else someone coughed.

"Can you hear me, Matt?" Carrie asked softly.

Her face swam in and out of focus. He moved his head
up and down. She placed her hands on either side of his
face, such gentle hands.

"How do you feel?" she asked.

His mouth moved, but no sound came out. He wanted to
say, "Fine, you can go now." He wanted to ask how long

she'd been there and how long *he'd* been there, but he couldn't speak.

"Never mind," she said. "You must feel awful. It wasn't the knife that did the damage, although that was no picnic, I know. The woman wasn't strong enough, fortunately, to get in very far. Unfortunately, the knife wasn't very clean, so you've got an infection." She leaned over him, bracing her arms on either side of the elevated hospital bed. "Does that make sense to you?" she asked, her hair cascading over her shoulders, filling his senses with the smell of honey and almonds.

Sense? Nothing made sense. Especially her being there. How did she get there? How did she know? Her hair brushed his cheek, as soft as a summer breeze. As if she'd read his mind, she explained.

"Buck called to tell me. I took the first plane. You scared us," she said, her voice shaking.

She was worried about him, he thought with wonder. So worried she came to see him. Six hundred miles. He hadn't even called her when she'd gotten hit on the head. He didn't deserve her. But since when was it against the law to want something you didn't deserve? There was so much he wanted to know. So much he had to ask. But all he could do was lie there and think.

Sometime later he was able to open his eyes a crack. He was alone. A tremor shot through his body. She'd left. She was gone. A nurse came in to take his temperature, and noted his inquiring look.

"She'll be back," the nurse said matter-of-factly. "I sent her down to the cafeteria to get something to eat. Didn't want to go, but I insisted. Even Florence Nightingale needed her nourishment."

Matt almost smiled. The poor woman didn't even know Carrie was a police officer. She thought she was a nurse. The woman made some marks on his chart, then she turned off the light and left. It was dark outside the window. Nighttime. How many nights had he been here?

This was the first one he was aware of. The door swung open and Carrie tiptoed into the room. Her smile illuminated the darkened room.

"You're awake," she said.

"I'm not sure about that," he said thickly. "Sometimes I have this dream..."

She sat carefully on the edge of his bed. "Tell me about it."

He shook his head. "Can't," he said. "You tell me... why... how..." Damn. The words wouldn't come. They were all there, backed up in his brain, waiting to tumble out, but his mouth just wouldn't move. If it did, he'd ask her... tell her... Yes, this time he would tell her everything.

What if it was too late? What if she'd found someone else? Maybe one of those abalone fishermen. He reached for her hands. No rings. Not yet. He fell asleep with her hands in his. If he held tight enough, she couldn't leave.

She did leave. But not for long. She always came back. She brought newspapers to read to him, food to feed him, and stories to tell him about what happened back in Moss Beach. She told him he was getting well. So well he could pay attention for at least ten minutes before he drifted off. He understood they'd found the right antibiotic at last, and the wound was finally healing. Best of all, he was able to think. Think about life, his life and her life.

The next afternoon she was reading aloud from the L.A. Times. First the headlines, then his horoscope. "The stars are telling you to examine what is working and what is not working for you," she said. "'Venus and Mercury play havoc with your love life. With your heart up for grabs, anything can happen.'" She paused. He looked up at her. She folded the newspaper.

He straightened his spine against the headboard, wincing as his bandage pulled at his skin. "Do *you* believe anything can happen?" he asked.

She pressed her fingers against his lips. "Before you say anything, I want to tell you you were right. About Moss Beach. I still love it there, but it really isn't me. Not without you."

"What are you talking about?" he demanded.

"About my job. About the town. After you left it didn' seem as interesting to me. Before it was just peaceful, then it got boring. Just the way you said it would." She drew a deep breath. "What I'm trying to say is that I miss you and I—I'm thinking of coming back to be your partner again."

He took her hand away from his lips and held it tightly in his. "I've already got a new partner."

Carrie felt her hopes deflate like a burst balloon. "Oh."

"So it wouldn't work. Besides, I don't think you've given it enough of a chance yet."

"Probably not," she agreed soberly as her spirits sunk to an all-time low. He didn't want her back anymore. It was too late. She should have known. She felt ridiculous for suggesting it, for taking advantage of his condition to be there at all. She pulled her hand from his and stood.

"Where are you going?" he asked.

"Home," she said. "To Moss Beach. To give it another try. Just like you said. Look—" she managed a faint smile "—you're almost well. You don't need me anymore."

"Wait." He rubbed at the dark stubble that lined his jaw. "I do need you. I've always needed you. I was just afraid. Hell, Carrie, I'm still afraid. I'm afraid I can't make marriage work. I don't know how. But I want to try. I have to try. Because this isn't working. My loving you and you..." He exhaled a ragged sigh. "I don't know how you feel..."

Carrie gripped the metal bedframe for support. Loving you. He'd said "loving you." The man who didn't believe in love. Who didn't think he knew how. Her knees threatened to buckle under her. She couldn't speak, couldn't tell him how she felt, not with her mouth as dry as cotton swabs. So she had to show him, gently, carefully, so as not to disturb his bandage. She eased back onto the bed and leaned forward. He was watching her, his eyes wary, waiting to see what she would do, what she would say.

She didn't say anything. She put her hands on his shoulders and met his lips, his warm, waiting lips. And put everything she'd ever felt, everything she'd ever wanted, into that kiss. She shifted her position, kneeling next to him, angling her head and kissing him again in case he didn't get the message. She broke away to catch her breath.

He was breathing hard, his eyes glazed, a slow smile creasing his face.

"Now do you know how I feel?" she asked.

"I'm not sure," he said, his eyes gleaming. "Could you repeat that once more?"

"*Mister* Graham," came a nurse's shocked voice from the doorway. "What is going on here?"

"I can explain," Matt said as Carrie pulled back with a guilty start. "This woman here—" he pointed to Carrie "—is my...my astrologer. She's predicting the future. And it looks promising."

The nurse shook her head and pulled out her digital thermometer.

"Don't bother," Matt said. "I can tell you right now I'm on fire. And so is she."

"Well," said the nurse, looking from Matt to Carrie. "It's catching. This is serious. Shall I call someone?"

"Call the mayor of Moss Beach, California. Tell her the wedding is on. Reserve the Delarosa House."

"Matt," Carrie said, bending over him. "Do you know what you're saying? Are you sure you're not delirious? Do you really want to get married?"

"Don't you?" he asked, the lines in his forehead deepening.

"Yes. More than anything." Her eyes misted. Was it possible? Could she have it all—Moss Beach, her house, Matt and a wedding in the historic mansion?

The mansion might have seen better days, but nobody alive that day would have believed it. It was a glorious fall day, the sky was an incredible blue, the breeze off the ocean was gentle. Carrie slipped into the dress that fit as if it was made for her. The white satin emphasized the smooth pale satin of her skin. The pearls on the veil had been stitched there one hundred and fifty years ago for another bride who, like Carrie, must have peered through the mist of white lace at her handsome groom waiting at the altar set up in the bay window of the enormous parlor. The guests turned their heads as the "Wedding March" began.

There wasn't a dry eye in the house as Carrie gracefully walked down the aisle, her head held high, her eyes riveted on her former partner and future husband. The man she'd loved since the first day he'd put his arms around her and taught her how to shoot straight.

When the mayor, as matron of honor, lifted Carrie's veil from her face, Matt caught his breath. She was so beautiful. Her hair gleamed red-gold in the afternoon sunlight, like a lucky penny. His lucky penny. Scenes of the past flickered through his mind. Yes, he'd taught her a few things, but she'd taught him much more. How to trust and how to love. How to believe in the future. He heard himself promise to love, honor and obey. Then he took her hand and they walked down the aisle. Together. The future was now.

The high school band assembled on the broad lawn and played their entire repertoire from marches to contemporary rock. The reception became a party for the whole town, to celebrate the reopening of the house as well as Carrie's wedding.

After milling through the crowd, accepting congratulations from at least one hundred people, Carrie sought out Matt who was leaning against a pillar that characterized the Spanish Colonial style of the house. He smiled when he saw Carrie approach and set down his champagne glass. Her gaze slid over his perfectly fitting tuxedo with the cummerbund around his waist. "Too bad about the ruffled shirt and tights getting lost, isn't it?"

He nodded. "The way things disappear around here." His hand slid down her back, across the tiny buttons and he let it rest on the curve of her hip.

"Like shoes and nightgowns," she said, her eyes lingering on his broad shoulders and his washboard stomach.

He grinned seductively. "Like we're going to do in about two minutes."

"What have you got against weddings?" she asked.

"Nothing. As weddings go, it's been fine. But I think we're going to like the honeymoon even more."

Epilogue

A year later a red-haired woman ambled down Main Street in the small coastal community of Moss Beach, California, pushing a baby stroller on a sunny Sunday afternoon. The hardware and the stationery store were closed, but the yogurt shop in the middle of the block was open, and the coffeehouse on the corner was doing a brisk business. As she approached, she could hear the strains of a classical concerto coming from the speakers in the small, warmly attractive shop and smell the rich aroma of freshly ground coffee.

She paused at the entrance, her eyes lingering on the polished surface of the gnarled redwood bar where patrons sat and sipped *latte*, espresso and cappuccino. The man behind the counter with his oxford cloth shirtsleeves rolled up above his elbows broke into a wide smile when he saw her and the baby. He leaned over the counter to blow the baby a kiss.

"Chloe, say hello to Daddy," Carrie instructed her, taking the baby out of the stroller. Chloe gurgled and cooed at the sight of her father.

Matt reached for her and held his daughter out in front of him to admire her fine red curls and her pink cheeks that matched her starched pinafore.

"That your baby?" a customer asked, looking at the two of them from over his steaming cup of Blue Mountain.

"Our baby," Matt said, exchanging a long look with Carrie.

The man looked around at the sleek counters, the roasted beans of every nationality displayed in huge glass jars, then gazed at Matt with undisguised envy. "You've got everything, man. Isn't there a law against that?"

"Ask the lady. She's the police chief around here," he said with a proud smile.

"No kidding? Why do they need a police chief in a place like this?"

"To make sure it stays this way. A good place to live and raise kids." A place to start over, to learn to live and love again. They called it Moss Beach, but he and Carrie called it a little piece of heaven.

It was time to put up the sign. The one he'd brought with him from over his office door when he'd left L.A. He'd repainted it to reflect his present outlook on life. Life's A Bowl Of Cherries. Somebody Else Removed All The Pits.

* * * * *

*Watch for the third in the "Miramar Inn"
series*—ALMOST MARRIED, *where Mandy
Clayton's sister Laurie finds a man of her own.*

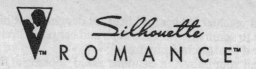

Silhouette

™ R O M A N C E ™

COMING NEXT MONTH

#1108 THE DAD NEXT DOOR—Kasey Michaels
Fabulous Fathers
Quinn Patrick moved in only to find trouble next door—in the
form of lovely neighbor Maddie Pemberton and her son, Dillon.
Was this confirmed bachelor about to end up with a ready-
made family?

#1109 TEMPORARILY HERS—Susan Meier
Bundles of Joy
Katherine Whitman was determined to win custody of her
nephew Jason—even if it meant a temporary marriage to playboy
Alex Cane. Then Katherine found herself falling for her new
"husband" and facing permanent heartache.

#1110 STAND-IN HUSBAND—Anne Peters
Pavel Mallik remembered nothing. All he knew was that the
lovely Marie Cooper had saved his life. Now he had the chance
to rescue her reputation by making her his wife!

#1111 STORYBOOK COWBOY—Pat Montana
Jo McPherson didn't trust Trey Covington. The handsome cowboy
brought back too many memories. Jo tried to resist his charm, but
Trey had his ways of making her forget the past...and dream about
the future.

#1112 FAMILY TIES—Dani Criss
Single mother Laine Sullivan knew Drew Casteel was commitment
shy. It would be smarter to steer clear of the handsome bachelor. But
Drew was hard to resist. Soon Laine had to decide whether or not to
risk her heart....

#1113 HONEYMOON SUITE—Linda Lewis
Premiere
Miranda St. James had always been pursued for her celebrity
connections. So when Stuart Winslow began to woo her, Miranda
kept her identity a secret. But Stuart had secrets of his own!

Take 4 bestselling love stories FREE

Plus get a FREE surprise gift!

Special Limited-time Offer

Mail to Silhouette Reader Service™

3010 Walden Avenue
P.O. Box 1867
Buffalo, N.Y. 14269-1867

YES! Please send me 4 free Silhouette Romance™ novels and my free surprise gift. Then send me 6 brand-new novels every month, which I will receive months before they appear in bookstores. Bill me at the low price of $2.19 each plus 25¢ delivery and applicable sales tax, if any.* That's the complete price and a savings of over 10% off the cover prices—quite a bargain! I understand that accepting the books and gift places me under no obligation ever to buy any books. I can always return a shipment and cancel at any time. Even if I never buy another book from Silhouette, the 4 free books and the surprise gift are mine to keep forever.

215 BPA ANRP

Name	(PLEASE PRINT)	
Address	Apt. No.	
City	State	Zip

This offer is limited to one order per household and not valid to present Silhouette Romance™ subscribers. *Terms and prices are subject to change without notice. Sales tax applicable in N.Y.

SROM-295
©1990 Harlequin Enterprises Limited

Become a
Privileged Woman,
You'll be entitled to all these Free Benefits.
And Free Gifts, too.

To thank you for buying our books, we've designed an exclusive FREE program called *PAGES & PRIVILEGES™*. You can enroll with just one Proof of Purchase, and get the kind of luxuries that, until now, you could only read about.

BIG HOTEL DISCOUNTS

A privileged woman stays in the finest hotels. And so can you—at up to 60% off! Imagine standing in a hotel check-in line and watching as the guest in front of you pays $150 for the same room that's only costing you $60. Your *Pages & Privileges* discounts are good at Sheraton, Marriott, Best Western, Hyatt and thousands of other fine hotels all over the U.S., Canada and Europe.

FREE DISCOUNT TRAVEL SERVICE

A privileged woman is always jetting to romantic places.

When <u>you</u> fly, just make one phone call for the lowest published airfare at time of booking— <u>or double the difference back!</u>

PLUS—you'll get a $25 voucher to use the first time you book a flight AND <u>5% cash back on every ticket you buy thereafter through the travel service!</u>